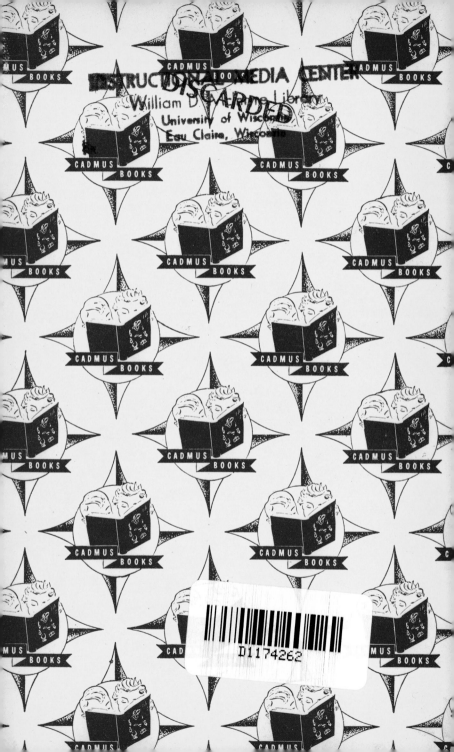

SLEIGH BELLS FOR WINDY FOOT

By FRANCES FROST

When you read this story you will have the feeling of Vermont winter, Christmas in the country, ponies, and the wonderful family to which Toby belonged.

Tish, a friend of Toby's is coming to Vermont with her father for Christmas. The preparation for Christmas, making the sleigh for Windy Foot to draw, buying the presents, and the terrifying experience of killing a bear, make a wonderful warm and happy story of Toby and his pony, Windy Foot.

* * * *

SLEIGH BELLS
FOR WINDY FOOT

SLEIGH BELLS
for
WINDY FOOT

by Frances Frost

Illustrated by LEE TOWNSEND

THIS SPECIAL EDITION IS PUBLISHED BY ARRANGEMENT WITH
THE PUBLISHERS OF THE REGULAR EDITION
WHITTLESEY HOUSE
McGRAW-HILL BOOK COMPANY, INC.
BY
E. M. HALE AND COMPANY
EAU CLAIRE, WISCONSIN

SLEIGH BELLS FOR WINDY FOOT
Copyright, 1948, *by the* McGraw-Hill Book Company, Inc.

PRINTED IN THE UNITED STATES OF AMERICA

Contents

Contents

1
Tish Is Coming!

ON Friday, the last day of school before Christmas vacation, Toby gazed dreamily out of the windows of the seventh-grade classroom. The bare branches of maples and elms lifted dark and motionless against a sky packed thickly with gray-white clouds. He wiggled restlessly, drew a picture of a wedge of wild geese inside the front cover of his history book, caught Miss Hunter's eye, and quickly put his pencil down in the groove at the front of his desk. Miss Hunter went on with the lesson in her pleasant voice. Toby forgot the classroom and turned his head once more toward the windows.

The village lawns about the white houses lay withered and rusty yellow; the leaves had long ago been raked to the roadsides and burned; and the only brightness was the dripping scarlet of the barberry bushes around the north side of the square. The bandstand in the middle of the square needed a new coat of green paint; it looked lonely, standing octagonal and peeling in the stretch of bronze grass under the silver day.

[9]

"Tobias Clark!"

Toby jumped to his feet in the aisle, blinking at the teacher. "Yes, Miss Hunter?" He swallowed. Miss Hunter was awfully pretty with her soft white hair and her amused, alert face, and her blue eyes; but she wouldn't stand for any nonsense, and that Toby knew too well.

"Will you answer the question, please?"

Toby felt his face growing red. Across the aisle, Dick Norton snickered behind his hand, reached out a stealthy foot and kicked Toby lightly in the ankle. Toby started, looked down at his ankle, looked up at Miss Hunter and stammered, "W-what—I'm sorry I don't know the question, Miss Hunter."

Miss Hunter's eyes turned into blue sparks. "Where were you, Tobias?"

The class giggled.

Toby's hands were perspiring. Then, before he knew what he was saying, he blurted, "It's going to snow, Miss Hunter!"

The class laughed out loud. Miss Hunter's mouth twitched; she glanced at the windows, nodded sagely, and agreed. "It certainly is. Snow for Christmas!"

Toby grinned with relief. "Boy, I was afraid it wasn't going to!"

Miss Hunter sobered. "My name is not 'boy,' Tobias."

"Excuse me, Miss Hunter."

"And the question was—do you know why the Pilgrims planted a great deal of corn in the spring of 1621? Virginia Higgins has suggested that they planted it to eat. That is the obvious answer but not the only one. Do you know?"

"It was the Indians," said Toby hurriedly.

"What about the Indians?"

"Well, that first winter—" Thank goodness he remembered reading this somewhere! "The Indians. I mean, so many people died that first winter that they were afraid the Indians would find out how few of them were left and would attack the settlement and finish 'em off, and so they planted as much corn as they could on the graves of the people to keep the Indians from knowing how many had died and they kept men tending the cornfields all the time so the corn would grow well and so there'd be men there all the time as lookouts. I mean," said Toby, taking a deep wavering breath, "I guess that's why they had so much corn for Thanksgiving and everything."

Dick Norton looked up at Toby with his mouth open and Toby whispered fiercely, "Flies!" and Dick shut his mouth abruptly.

"That's the correct explanation, Tobias," said Miss Hunter, making a mark in her recitation book. "You may sit down. And please concentrate on the lesson—not on the weather."

"Yes, Miss Hunter." He shivered slightly at his narrow escape. But how could he keep his mind off the weather when he'd been having fidgets for fear it wouldn't snow in time for the Christmas party? It would be terrible to have a green Christmas when Tish Burnham and her father, Jerry, were coming to visit the Clark farm for the first time.

Tish had run her black pony, Jigs, against Toby's Shetland, Windy Foot, at the Webster County Fair this last fall. During the Fair they'd become stout friends, and he'd been almost sorry when Windy Foot beat Jigs. Tish had told him she planned to put the prize money, if she won it, into her savings account toward medical college. Toby was still awed to think of a girl's wanting to be a doctor. But he bet she'd be a fine one!

He poked at the cover of his inkwell, saw Dick smirking at him, and discovered he was grinning at his own thoughts. He straightened his face and shook a promising fist at Dick under cover of his desk. Dick nodded and shook a friendly one back. Toby leaned his elbows on the desk and balanced his chin on the heels of his hands. Good thing Dick didn't know he was thinking about a girl. Would he get razzed!

When he and Dad had asked Tish and her father down to the farm for Christmas, Mr. Burnham had accepted. Tish's mother had died when Tish was four, and at times she and her father were pretty lonesome. Toby picked up his pencil and twirled it, listening for a minute to Miss Hunter.

"The Massachusetts colony—" said Miss Hunter.

"Aw—" thought Toby. He began to worry again.

Even if it snowed tonight, it might be all gone by Christmas Eve, which was next Wednesday. He glanced at the square-faced clock on the wall. Quarter of three. Hooray, only ten minutes left before the last bell! Miss Hunter closed her book and turned toward the blackboard.

Toby glanced once more toward the windows. The gray light was thickening. And there, down the road past the square, went a white horse, drawing a lumber wagon loaded with an enormous Christmas tree. He could wish on the white horse! He chanted silently to himself:

> *Lucky, lucky white horse!*
> *Lucky, lucky lea!*
> *Lucky, lucky white horse,*
> *Bring my wish to me!*

The only trouble with wishing on a white horse was that you couldn't look at him again or it would break the wish. He'd have to take a chance on it. He wished fervently that it would keep on snowing all during Christmas vacation. Then there would be enough snow for everything, skiing and coasting and snow fights— He shut his eyes tightly and quickly swerved his head away from the windows.

Miss Hunter turned around and smiled. She had printed on the blackboard in red chalk: *Merry Christmas to all of you and to your families!*

The class erupted into confusion and laughter and cries of, "Merry Christmas, Miss Hunter!"

The bell rang and Miss Hunter, her cheeks pink,

Down the road past the square went a white horse, drawing a lumber wagon loaded with an enormous Christmas tree.

called, "Run, children, run, or you won't get home in time for New Year's!"

Outside in the schoolhouse yard, Toby waited for Betsy, his little sister who had been nine in October and was now in the fourth grade. He watched the other school children piling into the school bus that went south down the valley, not north toward his father's farm. Just as Betsy came running up, he caught his breath in dismay.

"Toby! What's the matter?" Betsy grabbed his hand.

"Oh, darn it," he muttered. "I've gone and spoiled it!"

"Spoiled what?" she asked anxiously, gazing up at him, while her small brown pigtails flopped forward over her short blue Mackinaw, her head bare.

"Put on your hat—you'll catch cold," he told her with authority. "My wish. I wished on that white horse that it would snow all Christmas vacation and now I've looked at him again and spoiled it!"

"Maybe it'll snow just the same if it wants to," she said sensibly, pulling her knitted cap down on her head. Some wispy curls stuck out around the cap and made her narrow little face look perky. "Oh, Toby, it's the Christmas tree for the square he's got!"

The driver of the wagon had stopped the white horse near the south end of the square and was unloading the tall spruce tree from the lumber wagon. The white horse stood patiently, his head down.

"Come on!" cried Toby. "Let's see if we can help!"

They raced across the square. The elderly man, wiry but short, was having trouble with the heavy tree.

"May we help you?" asked Toby. "We're handy with trees."

"Sure thing," said the man. "You and the little girl grab a-holt of the top so the branches don't drag. I've got to get it over by the bandstand."

Betsy ducked into the branches at the top of the tree and lifted the tip, while Toby seized the trunk near the middle and the man lifted the heavy base.

"Okay," said the man cheerfully. "Let's go. If you have to let it down, yell."

It was a difficult load. Toby had forgotten to put on his mittens and the cold resinous trunk of the spruce bit into his hands. He held on grimly. He didn't dare turn to see how Betsy was making out. They reached the bandstand at last and the man shouted, "All right, let 'er down!"

Gratefully Toby emerged from the boughs, rubbing his sore icy hands together. They were smeared with pitch and smelled wonderful. But he didn't see Betsy. "Hey, Betts! Where are you?"

"Here," said her small voice, and he dashed back to the top of the spruce.

She was there, all right, sitting on the frozen ground, the top of the tree pinning her legs down, her feet caught in the boughs. "I slipped," she explained, "and I can't get out."

"Well, you can't sit there all night," said Toby gruffly,

relieved that she wasn't hurt. He lifted and tugged at the tree; the man came and helped him, and after several attempts they freed her.

She stood up, a trifle pale, her cap on the side of her head. Then she said, "Ouch!" and bent down and rubbed her shins.

"Betts!"

"I scraped me, that's all," she assured him.

"Thanks, kids," the man said and dug into his pocket and offered them each a dime.

"Oh, no, thanks," said Toby. "We were glad to help."

"Go on, take it," the man said. "It's Christmas, isn't it?"

"Yes, sir, that's why. We liked helping with the village tree. It makes it kind of feel like ours, too. When are you going to stand it up?"

"When I get the hole dug," the slim elderly man answered. "Well, thank you both."

"What's your horse's name?" Toby asked.

"Toby wished on him," volunteered Betsy, hopping from one foot to the other.

"Wished on him, eh? Hope you get your wish. His name is Chancey. You wouldn't know it to look at him now, but when he was a youngster, he took more chances on barbed-wire fences, ditches, and bridges, than any colt I ever broke." The man chuckled. "Won the pony race at the Webster County Fair when he was two years old!" he boasted proudly.

"He did?" Toby looked with admiration across the square at the old white horse.

"So did Toby!" declared Betsy. "This fall! On Windy Foot!"

"Oh, Betts, pipe down!" Toby was embarrassed.

"Good for you!" the man said. "What's your name? I didn't get to the Fair this year, but I heard about it."

"Toby Clark, sir. I didn't win the race—my Shetland pony, Windy Foot, did."

The gray-haired man looked him over solemnly. "Clark? Shetland pony? Hm-m. My grandson rode Chancey. The boy's dead now. War. But Chancey's still poking along."

"Windy's over in the livery stable—we drive him to school." Betsy seized the man's hand to keep him from feeling sad. "Would you like to see him on our way home?"

"That would be fine." The man smiled down at her. "I'll be here, digging that confounded hole."

"For gosh sakes, Betts," Toby said as they went toward the livery stable, "what's gotten into you today? You don't usually go around talking and bragging like that to strangers."

"Oh," said Betsy airily, tossing her pigtails back over her shoulders, "I got a prize in school today for a story I wrote. And I feel good. Don't be such an old fudge-busset!"

Toby howled with laughter. "Hey, you got that last word mixed! I bet it was some story!"

"It was," said Betsy calmly.

"What was it about?"

"A mouse."

"What was the prize?"

"I'm not going to tell you."

"Why not?"

"Nope." She shook her head violently.

"Why?"

"Because I'm going to give it to you for Christmas, that's why. Don't ask so many questions."

"Oh," he said meekly. "All right, Betts. But you shouldn't—you won it, whatever it is."

"Well, I'd rather you'd have it, and I can do what I want to, can't I?" She thrust her fists protectively into the pockets of her Mackinaw.

"Sure, sure," he said hastily, and had to grin, thinking he would never in this world understand girls, no matter whether they were nine years old like Betsy, or twelve and a half years old like Tish, or something or other like Mom.

Windy Foot heard them coming, and when they shoved back the livery-stable door he was stamping and whickering and whooshing and trying to shake his head loose from the halter.

"Hello, Windy!" Toby flung his arm around the Shetland's neck and stroked his nose. "Hold on—don't get so excited. Yes, we're going home. Stand still while I harness you." He backed the pony out of the stall while Betsy held up the shafts of the old light buggy.

The buggy had been too large for Windy, but Toby,

Windy was stamping and whickering and whooshing.

with Dad's help, had lowered and shortened the shafts to fit the pony, and Windy carried the children to and from school and on errands up and down the valley. Toby and Betsy and Johnny had painted the buggy a shining black with vermilion wheels, and Toby had bought a red whip—for decoration only. It jiggled gaily in the whipsocket by the dashboard and flaunted its bright tassel in the wind of Windy Foot's trotting. The red wheels and the red whip set off Windy's beautiful dapple-gray hide, and Toby was very proud of his equipage. He was the envy of the boys at school who had to ride the battered, noisy school bus.

Mr. Bronson, the lame livery-stable man, came out of his dingy office that reeked of horse blankets, venerable moth-eaten bearskin rugs, tobacco smoke, and the potbellied wood stove. Mr. Bronson himself smelled mostly of tobacco and wood ash and horses. His stable, these days, was haven for three horses besides the dappled pony and his own black mare, Miranthy. The only time Miranthy got any exercise was when cars became bogged down in springtime mud or winter drifts.

Mr. Bronson twitched his moth-gnawed Canadian cap sideways so that its visor stuck out over his left ear. "All set, kids? Vacation today, ain't it?"

"Yes, sir," answered Toby. "Begins today. We don't have to come back until the Monday after New Year's."

"Have a good time," Mr. Bronson said, lifting his

short nose toward the sky. "Smells like snow. Be bumped if it don't."

Betsy called, "Good-by, Mr. Bronson! Don't catch cold!"

"I won't! You neither!" he cackled, closing the stable door after them.

Toby leaned over and tucked the red Hudson Bay blanket around Betsy's knees. "You catch cold now and what'll Tish say?"

Betsy hugged herself with delight. "What day is she coming, Toby?"

"Wednesday morning some time—day before Christmas. Dad's got the train schedule." His heart did a back flip, a front slip, and started a jig in his chest. Four more days, and the fifth day would be Wednesday morning, and he and Dad would meet the Burnhams at the yellow-painted railroad station. Then, best of all, would come Christmas! He discovered that he was holding his breath and let it out in a great blast of white on the chill afternoon air.

In the square the tree man was working furiously at the frozen ground with a pickax. He looked up when Toby shouted, dropped the pickax, and came to the edge of the road.

"This is Windy, Mr.—Mr.—" Toby began.

"Name's Pete Hale," said the tree man, stroking Windy's neck. "He's a beauty and no mistake. Windy Foot?"

Windy shook his black mane and whooshed at Mr. Hale.

"He likes you," said Toby. "He never whooshes at people unless he likes them."

"Your name's Clark? You related to Jim Clark up the north valley?"

"He's my father."

"Your grandpa, Chris Clark, was a good friend of mine. Remember me to Jim. And have a good Christmas at your house."

"Oh, we shall! We've got company coming! You do, too, Mr. Hale!" Betsy beamed at him.

Mr. Hale touched his hand to his green-and-black checkered lumberman's cap.

Toby shook the reins on Windy's impatient back. "Dust, Windy. Merry Christmas, sir!"

As the pony swung away from the square the lights were turned on in the village. The store windows gleamed in the early dusk and threw topaz lights onto the irregular marble slabs that made up the sidewalks.

When they had passed the street lamps at the corners and the yellow lights glowing in the white houses beyond the wintry lawns, Betsy sighed peacefully. "I smell it," she said.

"What?"

"Snow."

"Me too," said Toby. He felt as light as a snowflake himself, and Windy's hoofs on the road clopped happily toward home.

2
Snowy Evening

THE snow began just as they drove around the curve by the ragged butternut trees and saw the lights of the farm up the valley. The flakes flicked gently on their cheeks and Toby could hear the first breath of the snow in the dry weeds at the roadside and over the brittle fields. He had been debating about stopping to light the lantern hung beneath the buggy but had decided that they would reach the farm before full night.

Johnny, looking like a demented gnome in his crimson snow suit, was dashing up and down the front yard, at one moment watching for them with his mittened hand to his eyes like a roly-poly Indian scout, the next moment rushing northwest into the growing flurries of snow with his arms spread wide. His face, under its red toque with the dangling tassel, was ecstatic as the flakes whirled into it, and he was shouting wildly to himself.

Toby stopped at the edge of the yard and let Betsy hop down. "Johnny!" he called. "Come and help me unharness Windy!"

The snow began just as they drove around the curve.

The five-year-old boy flung himself toward the buggy with a shriek. He scrambled in and plopped down beside his big brother, grabbing his arm. "Toby, let me drive the buggy in!"

"Here," laughed Toby, handing him the reins. "Easy, now."

"Naturally," said Johnny with dignity. He maneuvered the pony carefully outside the wagon shed and backed the buggy slowly. "There! Oh, Toby, it's snowing white, it's snowing fine, clear down to the Mason-Dixon line!"

They unharnessed Windy and led him toward the stable, pausing to let him have a drink from the water box. Windy shook his mane and whinnied at the snow. In the stable, Johnny filled the manger while Toby rubbed the pony down. Windy suddenly reached out and nipped Johnny's toque from his dark curls.

"Hey!" cried Johnny, startled. "You can't do that!"

Toby retrieved the toque and pulled it down on Johnny's head. "Scoot now and get ready for supper. I'm going to help milk. Windy, what're you feeling so frisky about? Christmas?"

Windy rolled his eyes.

"I bet," said Toby, stroking the sleek shoulder, "you think snow is ice cream!"

Immediately Windy cavorted and indicated that he most certainly did think so.

Toby laid his cheek against the Shetland's. "You just

wait—in the spring I'll give you some maple-sugar-on-
snow and that'll make your teeth stick together!"

Windy said he didn't want to wait till spring.

Toby chuckled, taking the lantern from its hook on
the wall. When he had given good-night pats to Jake,

the buggy horse, old sway-backed Serena, and the
farm team, Tillie and Tossie, he closed the stable door
behind him and lifted his own face to the flying late
afternoon. The flakes spun about the lantern glow as
he crossed the dark ground toward the highlighted
windows of the barn.

Ribs, the puppy, met him with a welcoming bow as
he slid the big door back only far enough to slip
through. The barn was warm with the smell of hay
and the breath of cattle, and mellow light fell from
the two lanterns hung on the whitewashed beams.
Cliff, the hired man, was pouring milk from a pail

into the strainer set in the top of one of the large cans.

Toby hung his own lantern on a nail. "Hi, Cliff, it's snowing!"

"Never saw anybody as crazy about snow as you are. Wait till you have to shovel it tomorrow morning!"

"I like to shovel it. Don't you?"

"Nope," said Cliff. "Can't say as I do. Gives me rheumatism."

Toby hooted. "Rheumatism, hah! After you've been pitching hay all summer and harvesting all fall, a little snow—"

"Gives me the creaks." Cliff turned back toward the stanchions. "You can shovel all you want to."

Toby reached for his milking stool. Dad came from the pens on the far side of the barn, looking anxious. "Hello, Dad. What's the trouble?"

"Hello, Toby. Georgette is going to calve in time for Christmas. Bad time of year. I wish cows would keep their calendars straight."

"Is she all right?"

"Yes, so far. What do you say I give the calf to Johnny for Christmas?"

"Oh, Dad, he'll love it!"

"That's settled, then," said Dad, his face clearing and his dark eyes shining in the lantern light. "Thought maybe you'd want it yourself."

"I've got Windy Foot!"

Dad put his hand on Toby's shoulder and shoved

him gently down the barn. "Let's get on with the milking. It must be nearly suppertime."

When the milking was over and they were walking across the whitened ground toward the woodshed, Toby said, "Dad, you know what?"

"No. What?"

"I think it would be wiser to give the calf to Betsy. Johnny's sort of young yet, and she'd be crazy about it."

"That's a better idea. Johnny can wait till his birthday in the spring to start his menagerie."

A sudden screech split the air and Cliff stumbled. "Barnacles!" he exploded. "That blithering cat!"

Poke, the black cat, spurted ahead of them toward the kitchen door. There she sat down and waited for them with an injured air, glaring at Cliff with her green eyes and lifting a front paw reproachfully.

"Toby, take my lantern." Cliff bent and scooped her up in his arms and stroked her indignant head. "There, Poke. I didn't mean it." Gently he rubbed her paw. "Why don't you watch where you're going and keep out from under my feet? Yes, you're a nice kitty. Oh, such a pretty kitty. Oh, purr, yourself!"

Toby laughed. "She sounds as if she had the croup."

"She's got an appetite, that's what," said Cliff, letting her down on the kitchen floor. She promptly skidded for her dish of food under the kitchen sink. All four paws were in excellent working order.

"Fool me, would you?" asked Cliff, trying to look mad.

Mom turned from the stove where she was making salt-pork gravy. Her short brown curly hair was ruffled and her cheeks were pink from the heat. "Toby, before you wash up, will you fill the wood box, please? And you'd better bring in some more logs for the fireplace, too."

"Is there time before supper?" he asked, sniffing hungrily.

Mom's eyes twinkled with amusement. "Plenty of time. You won't starve in ten minutes, will you?"

"I wouldn't be surprised if I fainted dead away right now."

"Well, I'd be surprised. A husky fellow like you."

"Aw, Mom." Toby grinned as he went back to the woodshed.

After the supper dishes were washed, they all sat around the fireplace in the living room and made plans for Christmas.

"Cranberries," said Mom, writing out her list of groceries to be brought from the village tomorrow. "Monday I'll start baking pies. Mincemeat I have down cellar. And pumpkin."

"Apple!" said Toby violently, hungry all over again at the thought of Mom's apple pies.

Mom looked at him without seeing him. "Cinnamon," she said thoughtfully, gnawing the end of her pencil.

"I'm all out of it. I always run out of something just when I need it."

Dad stretched in his big chair opposite Mom. "Mary, all right to get the turkeys tomorrow?"

Mom bobbed her curly head, frowning. "Wait a minute, dear. I forgot something. Oh, walnuts."

"What else can you think of that you want me to attend to, aside from your list there?" He smiled at Mom and she scratched her forehead with the pencil lead and smiled back, her brow smudged.

"Oh. The fruitcake's all made and ripening since Thanksgiving. Something. Don't ask me and I'll remember it."

"Mom's got a dirty face," warbled Toby gleefully.

"Who cares?" inquired Mom, writing again.

Betsy undid her arms from her knees, swiveled around from the fire and asked, "Why don't we start popping the corn and stringing it?"

On the floor, leaning against Cliff's shins, Johnny had been rubbing Ribs's ears. He jumped up so suddenly that he bowled the puppy over, hurled himself at Dad's knees. "Let's pop some popcorn, Pop!"

Dad shook him loose but held him under the arms and bounced him up and down on the oval rag rug. "You find the popper. Betsy, have we enough shelled corn in the can or had we better rub some more?"

"I'll go see. Johnny, come on." She seized his hand and they ran for the pantry.

While Dad balanced the handle of the open wire

shaker on top of one of the iron andirons, moving it quickly back and forth, Toby and Cliff grated the sharp-kerneled ears together and the corn rattled in the blue agate saucepans on their laps.

"This is tough on your hands," Toby said to everybody.

Cliff grunted. "Matter with you? This is soft as the driven snow."

Toby looked at Dad. The crisp smell of the popping corn filled the living room. "How about eating some? We don't have to string it all, do we?"

"Heavens, is your stomach a bottomless pit?" Mom asked, chewing her pencil again. "Ribbon candy if we can still get it," she muttered.

"Oh, can't we make fudge, Mom?" Betsy looked up from threading a large needle with white thread.

"Better double the thread, Betsy, and make the strings as long as possible. Yes, fudge. And stuffed dates. And peppermint patties with nuts. Toby, you'll have to crack a lot of butternuts."

"Soon as we finish this corn, Mom."

Dad emptied the first popperful of fluffy white corn into one of the big pans that they always used for sugar-on-snow. "How's that?" He reached for the popcorn can and emptied the last of the kernels into the shaker. "Start filling this up, Toby."

Toby poured his saucepan half full of kernels into the can and passed it to Cliff.

"Popcorn's pretty, popcorn's white."

Johnny trotted anxiously from one person to another. "What can I do? What can I do?"

"Don't lean on my popcorn arm," Dad said. "Shoo, Johnny."

"Here." Betsy handed the little boy a threaded needle. "Sit down and start stringing."

He plopped on the floor beside the big pan and shoved a small fistful of corn into his mouth. "Um. Good!"

"Don't eat it!" Betsy cried, sitting down beside him with her own needle and thread. "There won't be enough for the Christmas tree if you do!"

"I didn't eat much. Popcorn's pretty, popcorn's white, just like snow in the middle of the night!" Johnny threw another flake of corn in his mouth when Betsy wasn't looking.

"That reminds me," said Dad, glancing over his shoulder. "How's the storm doing?"

Toby arose and crossed the room. The windows threw yellow squares of light on the white earth and the stars of snow came whirling down, slanting from the northwest. "Looks about three inches deep already, Dad, and it isn't going to stop tonight."

"Tomorrow I'll go sliding middle-bump," stated Johnny dreamily. "Ow! Betsy, I stabbed me!"

"Let me see. Goodness, you're bleeding all over the popcorn. Come on and I'll put a Band-Aid on you."

When the two big pans were full of corn, all of them except Toby and Mom started stringing it. Toby had spread newspapers on the floor and was cracking butternuts on a flat field stone with the ball-peen hammer. Mom picked out the butterfly-shaped nuts. The apple and birch logs in the fireplace crackled brightly and Dad, leaning against the sofa while he strung corn, began to sing "Silent Night" in his deep bass. Cliff joined in with his tenor, Mom and Betsy sang soprano, Toby tried to hum alto, and Johnny chanted at the top of his lungs, completely off key. They laughed at him while they sang.

At nine o'clock, Mom interrupted the gaiety. "Time for bed, yoo-hoo!"

"Yoo-hoo," said Johnny, waking up suddenly from Cliff's right ankle. "You let me stay up an hour later and didn't even know it!"

"Oh, yes, I did," said Mom briskly. "But since this is the beginning of Christmas, I thought you might be allowed a little extra time for falling asleep right here. After all, we don't have school vacations every day."

Toby sighed. "We don't either, do we?"

"Sounds to me," said Mom, "as if you'd better take Johnny upstairs and fall into bed yourself. Betsy!"

Betsy blinked and opened her eyes wide, vaguely stabbing another white exploded kernel.

"Bed."

Betsy swallowed a yawn. "Oh, dear, I guess I'd better."

As they kissed Mom and Dad good night, Toby heard the snow flicking harder at the windows. He was going to get his wish on Chancey, the white horse, after all. It would be fine for skiing when Tish arrived. He climbed the stairs after Johnny and Betsy, and before he could stop himself, yawned loudly.

Johnny turned on the top step. "Toby Clark! You didn't put your hand over your mouth!"

Toby said sleepily, "That's right, I didn't. But I'm going to put a hand on you—"

"Eeek!" Johnny raced for the bathroom.

Toby laughed. "Betts, know what I was thinking?"

She shook her pigtails.

"Why don't we get the evergreens for the house tomorrow? And the princess pine? And how about partridge berries to hang with little red ribbons on the tree?"

"Partridge berries!" She looked up at him with admiration. "Oh, Toby, they'll be lovely! I know where there's a patch in the south woods. Not red—silver ribbon!"

"Okay, Betts. Silver ribbon." He bent down and hugged her. "Is this going to be a Christmas!"

In his own room he glanced around at the new drawings on his walls and wondered whether or not his work was getting any better. He got into his pajamas, rummaged in his closet, and brought out his two finished Christmas gifts. Here was a charcoal head of Jigs, Tish's pony, fixed and mounted in a seven-by-nine black ten-cent frame that he had found at the general store. When he bought it, the frame had contained a dreadful pinkish photograph of oranges. But now the narrow dull black set off Jig's good, intelligent head. Too bad she was so heavy in racing.

The second gift was a full portrait in pencil of Jerry Burnham's favorite mare, Golden Hind. Toby hoped that Tish's father, Jerry, would like his drawing. He held it off and looked at it again, put it on his chest of drawers, backed up and squinted. Well, the high lights were pretty good, but he hadn't quite caught the sense of flight in Golden Hind's amazing legs. When would he learn? How many years would it take him to put down the beauty of a horse? He felt like bawling with exasperation and impatience and at the same time realized that he couldn't, not when he was twelve and a half.

He'd put Golden Hind into a gray frame. Tomorrow he must remember to get white tissue paper and stickers and cards. He sat down at his desk to make out a list and his eyes kept shutting up on him. Finally he shoved up the window and thrust his head out, shivered with snow in his face, and took a deep breath of the slanting air. The snow was piling higher on his window sill. He swung around, snapped his light off, and made a dive for the bed.

The sheets were icy, but in a few minutes he had wound himself into a warm ball and begun to think once more about Christmas. He was half asleep when through his mind drifted a vision of Windy Foot pulling a sleigh. He sat up so violently that he rolled out

of bed and landed with a crash on the cold floor.
"Ethan Allen!" he exclaimed aloud to the darkness,
and shook his head.

He didn't wait to grab his dressing gown but shot
out of his room for the banisters, hopped up, and slid
to the bottom. Rubbing his back from its bounce against
the newel post, he loped into the living room.

Mom and Dad sat talking quietly, listening to the
turned-low radio. They looked up at him and smiled,
and glanced at each other.

"Well, good evening," said Dad. "What is it?"

Mom gave a short chuckle. "Must be important, the
way you hit that post."

Dad said, "Sh-h, Mary. History in the making."

"I don't doubt it."

Toby plunked on the floor at their feet. "Dad! Mom!
I just happened to think!"

"Yes," said Dad. "We heard you fall out of bed."

"Dad, you know that old sleigh hitched up on the
roof of the wagon shed?"

"I ought to, Toby. I hitched it there."

" Could I—might I have it? To cut down the way we
did the old buggy, to fit Windy Foot? So I can take
Tish for a sleigh ride?"

"It won't be an easy job, Toby."

"I know it, Dad. I mean, the more I try to figure it
out—"

"Want to do it yourself?"

"Yes, sir."

"Because I won't have time to help and neither will Cliff."

"If you'll tell me how you think I ought to go about it, Dad, please, I think I can manage it, I think—"

"All right. We'll unsling her in the morning after breakfast."

"Gosh, thanks Dad!"

"You're welcome." He reached for Mom's hand. "Think it's a good idea, Mary?"

"I think it's a wonderful idea. So will Windy."

"You need some sleep, partner," said Dad to Toby. "And don't fall out of bed again. You'll wake up the cows."

Toby hugged them both and went back upstairs, two steps at a time.

3
White Saturday

I T was still dark when Toby awoke. The alarm clock's illuminated face said that it was five o'clock. He lay snugly under the comforters, thinking about his Christmas presents for the family. Of the seven dollars and a half that he had earned helping Dad with the chores since the Fair, he had very little left. He had ordered a number of things from the mail-order catalogue: a doll carriage for Betsy; a set of targets for Johnny's BB gun; a Scandinavian hunting knife in a leather sheath for Dad; a nest of screw drivers for Cliff; a rubber bone for Ribs, the puppy; and a catnip mouse for Poke, the cat. For Mom he had made a foot-long candlestick from a four-inch-thick birch log, and tonight in the village he would buy three red candles to fit the three holes he had bored in it.

It would be terrible if the presents didn't come from the mail-order house in time. He now had a dollar and twelve cents left, and besides the candles he'd have to get tissue paper and stickers and cards and maybe some red ribbon. Oh, yes, and some silver ribbon for the partridge berries to hang on the tree.

It occurred to him suddenly that he didn't have a gift to send back to Billy Blue, the groom at Burnham's stable. Ho, he knew—he'd send him the drawing he'd done of Foxy Girl, one of Jerry Burnham's horses. He'd have to get a frame for Foxy tonight, too.

He hopped out of bed, said "Br-r-r!" and dashed to close the window. But then he stepped in a pile of snow under the window sill and gulped, "Oops!" It had snowed in deeply during the night. He snapped on his light and saw that the snow had piled high on his sill, too. Shivering, he scooped a fistful of the pure silver and ate it rapturously. When he had thrown the blown-in snow outdoors and wiped the floor, he closed the window and hustled to dress. The sky was full of stars now, but the whiteness had drifted at least a foot and a half. He'd have plenty of shoveling to do this morning.

The fragrance of coffee sailed up the stairs as he slid down. His stomach felt like a vacant lot. He told Mom so. She was setting the breakfast table.

"Have a cup of cocoa. Then you'd better help Dad and Cliff shovel out to the barn and the stable. They started an hour ago. Dad says it's two feet and more out there where it's drifted."

"Want me to fill the wood box first?"

"No, thanks, Toby. I have enough to last till after breakfast. Shovel first so they can get to the milking and you can feed the horses."

Toby hurried with his cocoa. "What're we having for breakfast, Mom?"

She laughed. "Sausage and pancakes. Suit your majesty?"

"You bet!" He hugged her and hustled out to the woodshed to get the extra snow shovel.

Poke definitely did not approve of the snow. She had little white shoes on her black paws and she high-stepped indignantly through the woodshed and demanded that he open the kitchen door. Toby bent and patted her and let her in. "Company for breakfast!" he called to Mom.

Cliff and Dad were shoveling toward the barn.

"Hi, Dad!" Toby said. "Cliff, I thought you didn't like to shovel."

"Don't," said Cliff, tossing a load of flying white sideways. "But if you're going to sleep all day—"

"I woke up as soon as I could." The air smelled wonderful. It was clear and cold and full of sparkles, and above the east mountain the morning star burned like a turquoise thistle.

"We'll finish this path," Dad said, "while you dig out to the stable, Toby, and attend to the horses and Windy. We'll do the milking and you dig the front path down to the mailbox, will you?"

"Sure, Dad." As he worked, enjoying the swing of his arms, the puppy pranced in the snow, became caught in a drift and wallowed, looking astonished. Toby whooped at him. When he was free in the path, Ribs snapped at a tossed shovelful of snow, getting his eyebrows and whiskers full of flakes.

"Woof!" he said hoarsely, his feelings hurt, and galloped toward the house.

"Woof to you!" called Toby cheerfully to Ribs's retreating tail.

After breakfast Johnny went coasting down the long path that Toby had shoveled from the house to the road. He sang wildly to the glittering day, even when he knocked the breath out of himself by plopping violently on his stomach on the sled.

Betsy wanted to set out on her snowshoes at once to gather evergreens up on the hill, but Mom said she'd better wait until Toby could go along to help. "Besides," Mom said, gazing critically into the oven, "I don't want you lost in a snowdrift."

"We'll go this afternoon, Betts," Toby promised. "This morning I'm going to start fixing up that old sleigh for Windy Foot. Want to help?"

"No, I guess not, thank you. I'll help Mom make fudge and things for Christmas."

"I know you, Betsy Clark—you'll clean out all the bowls and the icing bowls, too!"

Betsy flounced her pigtails. "Well, why shouldn't I, when I'm doing all the work, learning?"

"All the work like fun! Mom's doing the work and you're doing all the eating!"

Betts made a face at him, and he chuckled and tugged one of her pigtails. She chased him toward the door and he raced out to find Dad in the wagon shed.

Cliff was busy in the barn; so Dad and Toby worked alone. It took them half an hour to lower the sleigh from the rafters of the shed.

"Whew!" said Dad, brushing dust and cobwebs from his face. "I don't know how I ever got that thing up there."

The sleigh had once been blue, but the paint was cracked and peeling and the runners were a dingy yellow. Toby walked around it, trying to figure out how to cut it down to the proper size for Windy Foot. "Dad, what do you think I ought to do?" he asked finally. "The thills are too high up and the body's too far off the ground to fit Windy."

Dad lit his pipe, leaning against the green farm wagon. "I was thinking about it last night after you went back to bed. The only thing you can do to the body is to unbolt the runner supports and saw them all down evenly to the height you want. Then bolt them back, and lower the thills. Better get Windy out and try him in the thills before you fasten them again."

"Yes, Dad," said Toby uncertainly. "I don't know how well I'll do it, but I'll try. Thanks a lot." He considered the problem, gazing eagerly at the sleigh. "And then may I give it a coat of paint? I have some red and black left over from the buggy."

"Sure you have enough left? You'd better check and get more tonight if you need it." Dad pulled his mittens on. "You know the tools you'll need from the tool shed?"

"Yes, sir. The wrenches and the saw—"

"And the bits for making the new holes for the bolts. All right, Toby, get started. You have at least two days' tough work ahead of you."

By the time Betsy came to call him for dinner, Toby realized that he had chosen a difficult job. His hands were numb from working in the cold air and the frozen ground of the wagon shed had penetrated his heavy boots.

He had both runners off now and the body of the sleigh rested on the rusted earth, looking dilapidated and forlorn. He'd have to scrape the old blue paint off before he applied a new red coat. He'd checked his remaining cans of paint and knew he'd have to buy at least another pint of vermilion tonight. That would probably leave him about two cents for Christmas itself. Oh, well, he'd worry about that later. He shook his head and squinted at the supports.

"To-by!"

He jumped and banged his head on the underneath of the sleigh. "What, Betsy?"

"Mailman's come," she said.

He crawled out and said, "He has?"

"Nothing for you," she said smugly, "if that's what you're banging your head for. There was a package for Mom but she hid it in her own closet without opening it." She looked down at him shrewdly as he sat on the cold ground. "Why? You expect something?"

Why, thought Toby fiercely, did a boy have to be polite to little sisters? Or girls anyway? Why couldn't you just shake them? But you couldn't. And what would be the use, anyway? And anyway, they couldn't argue decently without getting mad—oh, barnacles! He sprang up and stamped his frozen feet.

"Are you, Toby? You expecting something?"

"Yes," said Toby shortly. "And when it comes, don't any of you dast touch it."

"Oh, no!" Betsy giggled. "Presents?"

"Never you mind," he said gruffly. "Curiosity killed a cat."

She skipped ahead of him up the path.

He tossed some snow at her. "Where's Johnny?"

"Dinner's ready," she said. "He's in the kitchen, thawing out. He ran into the mailbox post and knocked himself into a snowdrift."

Toby groaned. "I'll bet that stopped his singing for five minutes."

"Well, for a minute. But he didn't cry even though he skinned his cheek."

"My little brother," said Toby, wondering whether his feet would stay on long enough for him to reach the door, they were that cold.

"Well," said Betts shortly, "he's mine, too!"

"Yup," said Toby. "He's all ours."

"Phooey!" said Betsy angrily, holding the door open while he limped in. "Hurry up—don't let the flies out!"

Johnny was sitting in the tall-backed chair by the kitchen window and rocking Poke, who was complaining bitterly that she didn't like to be rocked. Johnny clutched her with firm arms and sang ardently, "Oh, Poke's the blackest cat in town and she got white when she sat down. Rockaby Pokey out in the snow, you should have seen her whiskers blow!"

"Yeow!" retorted Poke, and with a scramble she leaped from Johnny's arms and dashed under the stove.

"What's the matter with her?" inquired Johnny in an injured voice. "I was just trying to warm her up from the front yard. She got her feet cold."

Toby glanced at the large scraped splotch on Johnny's left cheek where he had connected with the mailbox post. "Maybe she wants to warm herself up. How's your cheekbone?"

Johnny straightened. "It's still there," he said, feeling of it and wincing a little. "Where'd you think it was?"

"On the mailbox post," said Toby, pulling his high

boots off and stretching his feet out toward the stove. "My feet are ice."

"Betts, please run up and get Toby's bedroom slippers," Mom said. "How'd the sleigh go, Toby?"

"Pretty slowly, Mom. I guess I can get all the sawing done this afternoon, though."

"No, you can't," Betts said, thrusting his slippers at him. "You promised to go up on the hill with me."

"That's right, Betts." He wiggled his toes toward the stove. "O-oh, this feels good."

"O-oh," said Johnny, climbing into his lap. "How many days before Christmas?"

"Four and a half before Christmas Eve. Hold still while I thaw."

"Me too," said Johnny, stretching his short legs out on top of Toby's long ones.

Dad and Cliff stamped their boots in the woodshed before they opened the kitchen door.

"Now that the snowplow has been through," Dad told Mom, "I guess we can all bundle up in the truck tonight. I've put the chains on."

"It'll be like a straw ride," Mom suggested, "if you put some straw in the back of the truck for people to sit on."

"I'll fix it," Cliff said, "and we've got plenty of horse blankets to wrap the kids in."

"Fine," said Dad. "We can do that Christmas Eve, too, when we go up to the carol singing at the tree in the village square."

"Oh, boy!" cried Toby. "I'd forgotten about the carols. And, Dad, I forgot to tell you yesterday—after school Betsy and I helped a man carry the tree to the bandstand. He said his name was Pete Hale and that he knew Grandpa Chris and he sent his best to you."

"Pete Hale? Of course I know him. Old friend of ours. Didn't he tell you I bought Windy Foot from him?"

"You did?" Toby looked for Betsy. "Hey, Betts, you hear what Dad said? No, Dad, he didn't tell us, but we showed him Windy and Windy whooshed as if he knew him."

Dad grinned. Cliff grinned. Mom looked stern, but the corners of her mouth twitched. "Dinner's ready. Johnny, did you wash your face and hands?"

"Look," said Johnny, holding out his hands toward Dad. "I'm as clean as snow, I am."

"You ought to be," said Betsy, hurrying to pat him. "You got enough of it down your neck."

"Yes, didn't I?" said Johnny cheerfully, ducking from under her hand and trotting toward the dining room.

Toby and Betsy exchanged glances which meant, "Uh-huh, our little brother."

Up on the south hill the snow lay heavily on the dark green boughs of spruce and hemlock, pine and fir. Silently Toby and Betsy snowshoed through blue shadows and brilliant patches of sunlight. They were too happy to talk. Looking around him, Toby thought of the art exhibition at the Webster County Fair and decided that he would try to do some landscapes in charcoal and in pastel. He'd enter them in next year's exhibit, along with his drawings of horses.

But he didn't have any pastels. He'd have to stick to his colored chalk, then. His chest felt about to burst with the beauty of the winter woods. He jumped when there came a sudden loud knocking over his head.

He looked up into the leafless boughs of an ancient oak and ahead of him Betsy turned back, staring upward.

Clinging nearly upside down to the old trunk, a three-toed woodpecker cocked his yellow-crowned head and surveyed them with bright eyes, then went back to his search for his grubby dinner, banging away with his sharp bill at the gray bark as if he were determined to split the whole tree apart.

Betsy's eyes were as black as the bird's when she whispered, "Look how his back shines!"

Toby nodded and grinned, signaling her to go on toward the clearing where they knew the partridge berries and the princess pine grew.

At the clearing they found the snow drifted deep and Betsy looked at him with dismay. "What're we going to do, Toby?"

He thought a moment. "Take off our snowshoes and use them for shovels." He bent and unfastened his straps, stepped off into snow up to his knees. "Hey, you'd better keep yours on—it's too deep. I'll dig and you can pick in the cleared places."

"It isn't as deep over there under those hemlocks— I'll look for princess pine and dig with my mittens."

"All right." He found it hard to shovel with a snow-shoe: the snow sifted through the laced thongs as fast as he lifted it up. He looked around for some wet snow, and found it where the sun was melting a patch farther on. He plastered the wet snow solidly on the thongs, stumbled back to the shadowy clearing, and waited for it to freeze. He watched Betts, squatted on her snowshoes, hauling princess pine streamers from under the hemlocks. Her cheeks were pink from exertion and the cold and he smiled fondly at her scrambling. Her blue cap had slipped sideways on her pigtails and she ate a handful of snow after she laid each string of starry green on her pile.

He hoped she'd like the doll carriage he was going to give her for Matilda, the doll with real hair and eyes that opened and shut, which Tish had won for her at the Fair. It wasn't an expensive carriage or a very fancy one, but from the picture in the catalogue, it looked as if it would fit Matilda all right.

He held one snowshoe up to the wind and found it frozen enough. He started shoveling diligently.

While they were both picking partridge berries and stowing the bright red bunches in their Mackinaw pockets, Toby suddenly glanced up and breathed, "Betts!"

There at the farther edge of the clearing, on the verge of the dark woods, stood a young fox, curiously unafraid, his fur golden russet against the snow, watching them with burning eyes.

"Oh!" gasped Betts, and the fox whirled and flew into the woods, his brush streaming behind him like a banner.

Toby sat down in the snow, his heart jerking crazily. "He wasn't afraid of us," he murmured.

Betsy gazed at him without saying anything and abruptly her eyes filled with tears.

"Oh, Betts!" He hurried to her and put his arms around her. Her narrow shoulders under the blue Mackinaw shook and she burrowed against his red-and-gray shoulder. "Please stop crying, Betts!"

"I'm not! I can't help it," she quavered. "He was so—so—"

"Yes, I know. Here, let me wipe your face. You'll get icicles."

She managed a shaky giggle and swallowed. "Toby—the way—the way he ran—like flying—"

"You stopped crying now?"

She bobbed her head, banging his collarbone even through his Mackinaw. "If I hadn't said anything, he'd have stayed."

"We saw him anyway." He gave her a gentle shake. "Come on, we've got to hurry. It's getting dark."

On the way toward the top of the hill, they loaded their arms with branches of pine and spruce. It was nearly dark when they reached the front yard and saw the kitchen lights gleaming on the white ground. They went around to the woodshed to take off their snowshoes and heap the evergreens on Cliff's own workbench by the far wall.

4
The General Store

THE truck bounced over the uneven slippery road and the tire chains clacked steadily toward the village. In the back of the truck Cliff and Toby, Betsy and Johnny, rode in the heaps of clean straw, beneath the warm blankets that smelled faintly of horses.

Toby lifted his head to watch the black tracery of trees against the wintry constellations and grinned at his favorite, Orion, the Huntsman, with his three-starred belt, his shield of the Pleiades, and his faithful Dog Star, Sirius, following him up the eastern sky toward the blue south.

Betsy sat close to Cliff, absorbed in her own thoughts, but Johnny, across from Toby, hugged his blanket around him and chattered as usual. Finally the little boy rocked across the truck and sat down heavily on Toby. "I'm asleep," he announced. Toby covered him with his own blanket and held him against his chest. "Sleep away, Johnny."

Toby turned his head to look north and saw the white road running backward, the naked trees against the white fields and the white hills, the Big Bear swinging low around the Pole. He began to whistle softly to himself, settling Johnny more comfortably in his arms. Johnny weighed a ton when he was asleep.

Cliff, who had wrapped part of his blanket around Betsy, nodded at him. Betts was asleep, too. "Nothing like stars," said Cliff hoarsely, "to make people decide it's night."

"What you want for Christmas?" shouted Toby above the racket of the truck.

"What I get," said Cliff, disposing of the subject.

Toby laughed inside of himself, wishing he could draw people so that someday he would be able to draw Cliff's lean weather-wise face. It was patient, tolerant of weather and kids, with fiercely squinting blue eyes that could laugh when Cliff's features were perfectly straight. You couldn't fool Cliff for a minute, although he pretended to let himself be fooled for the fun of it. All the Clarks and all the animals loved him, but could they let him know it? Not Cliff. He'd simply walk off and start building something, useful or foolish—it didn't matter. Or stand in the middle of a field and measure the weather, any time of year. Toby gave a weak whistle and subsided. They were coming into town.

The tree in the village square was tall and beautiful with its colored lights, and Toby shook Johnny awake to look at it. Dad stopped the truck in a vacant space near the general store and everybody piled out. Sleighs and cars and trucks and sledges were parked all around the square.

Any time of year, the village general store was wonderful. It had everything you could think of, and Mr. Mike would think of it while you were trying to think of it, even if he didn't have it. If he didn't have exactly what you wanted one week, he'd have it a couple of weeks from then; you could be sure of it. Mr. Mike never forgot. He remembered every single child from away back when he first came into the store and quavered for a piece-peppermint-please until he stalked in like Toby, feeling sure of himself and herding Betsy and Johnny ahead of him, to buy Christmas presents. Mr. Mike's real name was Michaelis, and he'd come down from Canada years ago, as his white head attested. His English wasn't what it might be cracked up to be, but nobody cared. Mike would give you a rake or a bag of seed or a bolt of cloth for clothes for kids, as you needed them, and you could pay him when you got around to it. He trusted the valley and the valley trusted him. The Clark family had relied on Mr. Mike more times than once. Aside from that, they liked him and Mrs. Mike, and the Mike children who were between the ages of Johnny and Betsy.

"Never had time," Mike always said, "to get a family until hair turns white. But we are all young together." And he and Mrs. Mike and the three children would smile at one another. It made Toby feel warm inside.

Tonight the store was crowded and gay and filled

with the excitement of Christmas. Mr. Mike was at-
tending to the grocery department, Mrs. Mike was
measuring cloth, and there were a couple of assistants,
both high-school students, who were helping out with
the various counters.

Toby let go of Betsy and Johnny and they darted
off. He wandered around, smelling the store. It smelled
of leather and cloth, of coffee and spices, of grain and
pickles. While Mom, looking distracted, ordered her
groceries, Dad bought the turkeys. Toby tried to see
where Johnny and Betts were, but people got in his
way; so he ambled, slipping between men and women
and young ones as he gazed at the rainbow colors of
the loaded counters.

"Hello, Toby," said Mrs. Mike. "Need help?"

"Hello, Mrs. Mike. I've lost Betts and Johnny."

"They're around somewhere," Mrs. Mike assured
him. "They can't get lost in here."

"No, I guess not," he said gratefully. "Gosh, the
store looks pretty."

"We decided to decorate it this year a little bit.
Papa," she lifted her chin toward the grocery depart-
ment, "is crazy about Christmas. May I help you, Mrs.
Bedeaux?"

Toby looked at the bright bolts of cloth, at the
gleaming milk pails and sap buckets, at the shining
leather of harness, the red of the coffee grinder and the
green tin of the spice bins. And above them all, Mr.
Mike, Mrs. Mike, and the three young Mikes, no doubt,

had swung streamers of green and red raffia holding up an enormous red paper bell. He could almost hear the bell ringing with the joy in the hearts of the Mikes. Oh, gosh, he thought, what was I going to buy? I bet I forget half of it.

He purchased the three red candles for Mom's birch-log candlestick, red tissue paper, a box of stickers and a box of gift cards, a ten-cent frame for the drawing of Foxy Girl for Billy Blue. There was something he'd forgotten and he shook his head, but it was off some-where. He had fifty-two cents left and when he'd bought a can of vermilion paint for the sleigh, he had exactly twenty-two cents left.

He saw Johnny talking earnestly to Cliff and saw Cliff lift him up at the stationery counter. Johnny pointed and Cliff nodded and put him down. Dad had given Johnny and Betsy a dollar each to spend for gifts. While Toby was trying to make up his mind whether to spend the twenty-two cents now or to save it to buy Tish a hot fudge sundae sometime after she got here, Johnny seized his hand.

"Toby, please come help me."

"Sure, Johnny. But wait till I go put my packages in the truck. You stay here and I'll be right back."

He hurried out into the crisp night and shoved his things under the straw in the left-hand corner of the truck. When he returned, Johnny was standing on tip-toe at the perfume counter.

"I want one of those little bottles," said Johnny,

hitting the floor with his heels. "Please, Toby. For Tish. Is there one that says violets?"

Toby searched, picked out a vial, and handed it to him.

Johnny sniffed it critically. "Uh-huh." He jiggled the money in his mitten. "How much is it?"

"Ten cents."

"Please pay the lady for it, Toby. I can't reach."

Toby paid Mrs. Mike, thinking that if Tish ever used it you could smell her a mile away. Mrs. Mike's amused eyes agreed with him. "What next?" asked Toby.

"For days and days I've been thinking and thinking. I want a powder puff for Mom."

"Okay. Over here."

Johnny selected a violently pink puff wrapped in cellophane. "It glitters nice, doesn't it, Toby? Lookit the way it shines! Will you help me wrap up my presents? Because if you don't, I'll have to ask Betsy and she's awful fussy about where you put stickers and things."

"Stickers—phoo," said Toby. "As long as they stick, who cares where?"

"Uh," said Johnny somberly. "That's what I think. Only they never stick. I don't sit on 'em long enough. I want some ribbon for Betsy's pigtails." After much deliberation as to color, he chose a yard of narrow blue ribbon. "That's pretty, isn't it? And a jackknife for Dad."

"These ten-cent knives aren't sharp," Toby warned.

"Dad always sharpens knives," said Johnny calmly, "whether they're sharp or not. Lift me up, Toby. I can't see."

"Oh, gosh," said Toby, "you're getting heavy."

Johnny grabbed a small knife with a bone handle. "This. And some of those green ear muffs for Cliff."

"All set. What next?"

Johnny bought a couple of other presents, and Toby was getting a little tired of following him around. All of a sudden he noticed Cliff and Betsy, a couple of counters over. Cliff had one arm loaded with packages and at the hosiery counter he was looking down at Betts, his lean brown face crinkled with trouble. Betsy's face was beginning to pucker.

Toby grabbed Johnny's hand and hurried over. "What's the matter, Betts? Cliff?"

"I haven't got enough money!" she wailed. "I want to get Dad that pair of plaid socks and they cost thirty cents and I've only got ten left!"

Cliff looked startled. "Is that all? I didn't know what ailed you. Barnacles on a bulrush! Here." He started to reach into his pocket.

Toby shook his head. "Here, Betts, I've got it. How do you think Cliff's going to have time to buy his own presents if he has to tow you around all the time? Come on, here's the twenty cents and here's a clean handkerchief and blow your nose." He had to grin up at Cliff. "Well, I've two cents left after all. It's what I figured."

"Barnacles," said Cliff, his face stricken. "You that short just before Christmas?"

On the way home, Johnny sat in the front of the truck with Mom and Dad. He leaned against Mom and yawned. "I'm kind of sleepy again."

"You ought to be," said Mom, wrapping a blanket around him. "It's a long way past your bedtime."

"Naps!" said Johnny. "That's all I do. Wake me up when we get home, Mom."

"I wouldn't think of it," said Mom. "Are you all right back there?"

"Fine, Mom!" called Toby.

"Well, just don't go to sleep on everybody's presents!"

"I got the two of 'em on either side," said Cliff. "They can't move from here. Home, James."

"Why, Cliff," laughed Mom, "you sound as if you were riding in a limousine."

"Well, I ain't," said Cliff. "My bones got a feeling that this is going to be a first-rate Christmas. That's all. And that's enough."

"Me, too," said Toby dreamily above the rattle of the truck. "My bones do, too." He could feel Cliff's collarbone through their Mackinaws and it felt good and solid.

5

The Red Sleigh

IT took Toby part of Sunday and most of Monday
to finish the sleigh, and the paint wasn't dry until
Tuesday morning. The minute his chores were
done on Tuesday, he wanted to try out the sleigh with
Windy Foot, but decided to wait until after the mailman came. He peered impatiently through the kitchen
window. What if the package didn't arrive from the
mail-order house in time? He fidgeted around the
kitchen until Mom asked, "For heaven's sake, Toby,
what's the matter with you?"

He told her. "It will be awful if the things don't get
here for Christmas."

"Don't worry—there's still tomorrow." She was icing
a chocolate cake. "Want to clean out this icing bowl?
It'll take your mind off your troubles."

"Do I? M-mm," he said. "Mom, you make the best
icing in the world."

She made a mock bow. "I thank you, sir. It's nice
to be appreciated. And you may fill up the wood box
again, if you please."

He watched toward the road over the scarlet geraniums on the window sill as he scraped the bowl. "There he is now, Mom!" He shoved the bowl onto the table and dashed out of the door and down the path where Betsy and Johnny were coasting.

But the mailman handed him only a batch of square envelopes—Christmas cards.

"No package?" he asked.

"Nope," said the mailman, shifting the boxes piled on the right side of his seat. "Not today, Toby. You expecting something?"

"Yeah, Mr. Bean. Christmas presents for the family."

"Hope it comes tomorrow, then. No delivery Christmas Day. I'll keep an eye out for it."

"Thanks, Mr. Bean."

The mailman started his car. "Looks like more snow. See you tomorrow."

Toby hadn't noticed it, but it did smell like snow again. As he went back toward the house, he had to step into a drift to get out of the way of Johnny and

Betsy whooping down the slope on one sled. Johnny was sitting in front, Betsy behind, and she was steering.

"Whee!" she yelled and waved at him and steered at once into a snowbank.

The sled turned over, spilling both of them.

Johnny sat up, wiping snow off his face. "Betts, why don't you watch where I'm going?"

"Well, I went, too, didn't I?"

Toby stood in the drift, glancing over the mail. "Here, Johnny, something for you. From Tish. And you, Betts."

"Me?" Johnny skidded, recovered his footing, and made a dive.

"Whoa," said Toby. "Here you are."

Johnny took the envelope and stared at it. "You'd better open it for me, Toby. You know I can't spell yet."

"You open it and I'll read it for you." Toby plowed out of the drift onto the path. "Here, Betts."

Betsy sat down on the sled to read her card.

Johnny exclaimed, "Oh, look at the little angels singing! What's it say, Toby?"

"It says, 'Hope you're practicing up on some songs to sing at Christmas. Love, Tish.'"

"Oh, I am!" cried Johnny, seizing the card and gazing at it. "I'll sing and sing and sing—"

"You'd better start making up some special ones," said Toby, going toward the kitchen. He had a card

The sleigh was a little slab-sided, but it was beautiful.

from her, too, but he wasn't going to read it out here. He stuffed it in his pocket and took the rest of the mail in to Mom.

He hurried out of the back door to the woodshed, pulled the envelope from his pocket, and ripped it open. The card was an etching of the Brooklyn Bridge in New York and the message said, "Can't wait till Wednesday to see you all again. Billy Blue sends his best. Sincerely, Tish."

Toby put the card back in his pocket, making sure it wouldn't get bent, and began to whistle as he gathered up an armful of wood for Mom's wood box.

When he had harnessed Windy Foot, he led the pony to the wagon shed and backed him between the thills of the gleaming sleigh. He'd painted the body vermilion, the runner supports black. The sleigh was a little slab-sided but it was beautiful. So was Windy, for that matter, in his shining black harness, with his black mane and tail and his sleek dappled-gray hide. Toby stood back against the old wagon and admired the pony and his work; and suddenly feeling full of hilarity, he began to sing loudly, "Good King Wenceslas looked out, on the feast of Stephen!"

The newly shined runners slipped smoothly over the snow as he drove out to the barn. The sleigh tipped to starboard where he'd sawed the supports a bit unevenly, but that didn't matter too much. He'd bolted them back good and hard. The only thing was, it made him mad at himself for not doing a perfect job. Windy didn't seem to care. He tried to look around at Toby and shook himself in his harness.

Toby called to Dad and Cliff. "Come on out and look at us!"

Cliff came, a pitchfork in his hand. "Your father's busy with Georgette. My, you look mighty set up."

"Doesn't Windy match the sleigh?"

"Yup," said Cliff. "But you forgot something."

"What?"

"Bells." Cliff was in a hurry. "Seems to me there used to be a mess of 'em somewhere in the tool shed. You'll have to clean the rust off."

"I will! This afternoon! Cliff, I'm taking Windy for a run up to the village so he can get used to the sleigh. Anything you or Dad want?"

"Wait till I see." Cliff disappeared into the barn.

Windy stamped in the trampled snow of the barn-yard and flung his head up toward the northwest. Toby glanced at the thick gray-white snow clouds massed over the mountains and sniffed the chill sweep of the wind. He was certainly getting his wish for snow that he'd wished on the white horse, Chancey. He hoped Tish wouldn't forget to bring her skis. She could use Mom's snowshoes, but everybody else's skis except his own would be either too long or too short for her.

Cliff returned and said that Dad would like him to get a sack of chicken feed at the general store and charge it. Cliff handed him five dollars. "And he says to stop at the livery stable and pay Mr. Bronson for the rent for Windy's stall since September." He gave him another dollar. "And he says here's your pay for last week and this week in advance in case you want to get something more for Christmas."

"Thanks, Cliff." Toby flapped the reins on Windy's back. "Okay, Windy, dust!"

Windy raced out of the yard and down the road, the sparkling sleigh reeling behind him. Toby laughed with delight, and shouted all the Christmas carols he knew at the top of his lungs the entire way to the village.

That afternoon he found the rusted bells on a beam in the tool shed and scrubbed them until they glittered. He fastened them to the shafts of the sleigh and shook the thills up and down to hear them jingle. He felt very proud of himself.

Whistling, he cleaned and polished the family sleigh so that it would be ready tomorrow morning when he and Dad would go to the station to meet Tish and Mr. Burnham. The family sleigh was a big double seater, green with yellow runners. It gleamed in the shadows of the wagon shed when Toby walked out into the early dusk. The air was filled with slanting crystal flakes. He met Dad coming into the yard with the Christmas tree, a fine tall spruce. Johnny and Betsy tagged after him.

"Dad! Why didn't you tell me you were going up on the hill, so I could help?"

"I knew you were busy with the sleighs. Anyway, I had two good helpers here. Betsy, give Toby the ax. You've carried it long enough."

Johnny was so tired that he staggered. "We got a great big Christmas tree—Dad and Betts and Dad and me!" he warbled, but his voice was muffled with exhaustion. "Pfoo," he said, stumbling over Toby's feet. "I can't see straight."

"I should think you can't. You pop in and take a nap before supper."

"Naps!" said Johnny scornfully, coming to life. "That's all I ever do. I'll be glad," he added grimly, "when I get grown up and then I won't sleep again, ever."

Dad chuckled. "You go on in and see Mom, Johnny. And, Betts, you go up in the attic and find the tree decorations."

Betsy seized Johnny's hand. "Where'd we store them, Dad?"

"Don't ask me. Mom knows. I've got to put a base on this tree."

"I'll fix the base, Dad," Toby offered. "You must be kind of tired."

Dad let the tree down in the woodshed yard. "Tired? Haven't time to get tired. All right, you fix it and help Mom while I go out and see Georgette and start milking."

"Oh, Dad, is it the ten-o'clock train the Burnhams are coming on?"

"That's what Jerry wrote me. We'd better start from here around nine, just to be sure." Dad strode off toward the barn.

Toby hummed happily while he fashioned the base for the spruce tree. Ribs bowed around and around him, approving of the humming with short barks. "You crazy dog," Toby said affectionately, pausing to give Ribs a rub behind the ears.

Ribs wagged himself nearly out of his tail, woofed hoarsely at the falling snowflakes, and lay down in the woodshed doorway, most certainly out of breath, and watched Toby with adoring dark eyes. Poke appeared from somewhere, examined the tree, and went to lie down beside Ribs. He reached over and nuzzled her, his tail thumping. Poke waved a paw at him, arose, and went to the far side of the doorway and folded her front feet under her chest.

As he hammered, Toby began singing an old sledge-hammer song that Cliff had taught him when they were mending fences in the spring:

> *Put 'em up solid, they won't come down!*
> *Hey, ma laddie, they won't come down!*

Ribs moaned and Toby laughed and started a ballad that Cliff liked to sing when he was feeling good:

> *I used to have an old gray horse,*
> *He weighed ten thousand pounds,*
> *Every tooth he had in his head*
> *Was eighteen inches around.*

That horse he had a holler tooth,
He could eat ten bushels of corn,
Every time he opened his mouth
Two bushels and a half were gone.

I'm a-goin' down to town,
I'm a-goin' down to town,
I'm a-goin' down to Boston Town,
To carry my milk cans down!

Ribs howled mournfully. Toby gave the base of the tree a final whack and set it up. Yes, it was on even keel. He put the tools away and carried the tree into the house, accompanied by Ribs and Poke.

"Hello," said Mom, coming out of the pantry. "Oh, what a beauty of a tree!"

"Where do you want it, Mom?"

"The same place—in the corner at the right of the fireplace. Betsy's up in the attic hunting for the things —we'll decorate it after supper."

Toby placed the tree carefully in the living-room corner. It was strange how a tree was even more fragrant indoors than in the woods. He went to scrub his hands and had a hard time getting the spruce pitch off. It would simply have to wear off. He checked the wood box, brought in more logs for the fireplace, and sprinted for his room. There was time enough before supper to do some sketching.

With his soft 6B pencil, he began a drawing of the woods on the hill as he remembered them from Saturday afternoon when he and Betsy had gone up for the partridge berries and evergreen branches. He was completely absorbed in his drawing when Johnny banged at his door and came in without waiting to be answered.

"What are you doing, Toby? Mom says come to supper—she's called you twice."

"Oh, I didn't hear her—I'm sorry."

"Please hurry up. My stomach is sticking to my wing bones. Oh, Toby, that's a nice picture."

"It isn't finished," said Toby, pleased at Johnny's admiration of his work. "Come on, I'll show you how to slide down the banister."

"You watch me, Toby, and don't let me fall!"

"I wouldn't let you fall for anything," Toby answered, holding on to the little boy and easing him down the banister rail. "Think I want you to break your wing bones?"

"Make me bang on the post the way you do!"

Toby let him bang gently.

"Whee!" exclaimed Johnny, his eyes shining with delight as Toby lifted him down. "Someday I'm going to bang that post right off!"

"I don't doubt it," said Toby. "Scat, before you starve."

6

The Day before Christmas

Wednesday morning Toby woke up on the floor, fighting his way through a snowdrift that he had snagged his skis in. Betsy was holding down his feet and Johnny was bouncing on his stomach and both of them were howling, "Hark, the Her-ald Ang-els Si-i-ing!"

"Barnacles!" said Toby, blinking. "How'd I get here?"

The blue light outside the window said six-thirty at least. Milking! Shoveling! He'd overslept all right.

"We don't know how you got here," said Johnny sympathetically, "but we heard you. You were yelling."

"You must have hit your head on something," said Betsy, letting go of his feet. "Anyway, we came running. Are you all right?"

"How do I know until I wake up?" inquired Toby fuzzily. "Johnny, get off my stomach till I see."

Johnny stood up and they both watched him anxiously as he struggled to his feet and felt of his head. "Bump is all. I was dreaming. I thought I was skiing."

"Well, you certainly were thrashing when we got

here," Johnny told him with a giggle. "Like to wake the dead."

"What dead?" asked Betts impatiently. "He's awake now. Toby! Today's the day before Christmas!"

Toby looked down at her and grinned foolishly. "Huh? Come again. What day?"

"Wednesday! You've got to meet Tish!"

He rubbed the back of his head. "Wednesday! Oh, my gosh!"

"I shut the window," Betts said. "Toby, are you awake?"

Abruptly he was galvanized into action. "Sure, I'm awake. Tomorrow's Christmas! Scoot, kids! Get dressed, and thanks for waking me up!"

"If you hadn't fallen overboard," said Johnny conversationally, "we'd never have known you'd oversleppen."

"You made an awful racket," said Betts, going toward the door but looking back over her shoulder. "Are you *sure* you're all right?"

"Yes, thanks, Betts. Race you both downstairs, fully clothed!"

"No!" Johnny shrieked. "I can't button as fast as you can!"

"Yes, you can, too," said Betts. "Come on, I'll help you."

All three of them, dashing from their rooms, met in a collision at the head of the stairs. They burst into laughter. Johnny went tumbling and Toby dived for him, picked him up and sat him astride the banister.

"This time you slide alone."

"Who, me?" Johnny's freckles became suddenly very prominent. But he grasped the rail with both hands.

Toby raced to the bottom of the stairs. "Hold on, Johnny, I'll catch you!"

Betsy stood at the newel post and shouted, "Slide, Johnny! I'm a cushion so you won't bump!"

"I want to bump!" yelled Johnny and slid perfectly to the post, ending up against it with a soft thump. "Oh," he beamed. "I hit it. Help me down, please."

"Nice going," said Toby, hugging him. "I've got to run—I'm late for milking."

As he loped toward the kitchen, he heard Johnny asking Betsy bitterly, "How old do I have to be before I can go milking, too?"

And Betts replied, "A couple more years, Johnny, and you'll be able to lick your weight in wildcats, I hope."

"I can lick my weight in wildcats right now," stated Johnny with a quiver of doubt in his voice. "I slid down the banister all by myself, didn't I?"

Toby laughed, kissed Mom's cheek quickly, said, "Sorry, I must have been sleeping," and hustled toward the woodshed door.

"Wood after breakfast!" Mom called after him.

"You bet!" he shouted back and immediately realized that he was shouting to the new snow and the white hills and the white roof of the barn and to the day before Christmas. "Oh, glory," he said softly to himself as he opened the barn door.

The ten-o'clock train was late. Toby and Dad sat in the front of the double-seated green sleigh and waited.

Dad puffed comfortably on his pipe. "Toby," he said after what seemed to be an hour, "go and check again with the ticket man, will you?"

Just as he climbed down from the sleigh, the train whistled far up the track. "It's coming, Dad!"

Dad grinned at him. "Sounds like it. And you look as if you were going to explode. Take it easy." He left the sleigh and stopped to pat Jake, the family driving horse. "I should have put a blanket on you," he said, "but it won't be long now before we start for home."

Jake rubbed his nose against Dad's dark green Mackinaw and his breath steamed white in the sunny air.

Toby thought of the mailman. What if his package didn't come today? He'd have to do some fast inventing for everybody. He forgot the catalogue presents as the train steamed in, puffed and slowed and stopped. He was glad that Dad had a hand on his shoulder.

There they were! The conductor was helping Tish down from the third coach, and behind her Jerry Burnham in a gray Mackinaw waved skis at Dad.

The train steamed in, puffed, slowed, and stopped.

Dad took his hand off Toby's shoulder and gave him a slight shove. Toby ran.

"Merry Christmas, Tish! Merry Christmas, Mr. Burnham!"

Tish smiled warmly and held out her hand. "Hello, Toby."

Dad and Jerry Burnham thumped each other.

"Here, Tish," said her father, "take your skis while I get the suitcases off."

"Let me carry the suitcases, Mr. Burnham." Toby felt shy all of a sudden. He had to do something quickly. He carried the suitcases to the sleigh.

"You young ones sit in the back," said Dad. "I'm glad you could make it, Jerry. Family's been in a stew for weeks."

Jerry Burnham got in beside Dad with a ghost of a grin. "So has this family."

"Even Georgette," said Dad.

"Who?"

"One of our cows," said Dad, "is celebrating. She thinks she's going to calve today."

"What a time of year for a cow to celebrate!"

"Comes in handy for a Christmas present, though." Dad unwound the reins from the whipstock. "All right, Jake. Home."

Toby and Tish settled in the back seat with her skis on Toby's side, their feet on the suitcases, and the old brown bear rug over their knees.

Tish was wearing a black ski suit with white mittens

and a white cap, and her eyes were shining. "How are Betts and Johnny?"

"Loopy," said Toby happily. "As usual. They're probably wearing out the front yard watching for you."

Tish looked directly at him. "You mean it?"

Toby's shyness evaporated. "You bet I do. We've been afraid something would happen so you couldn't make it. How's Jimmy Slater?"

"Jimmy's same as usual. I haven't seen him since the last day of school but he said to tell you Merry Christmas in case he didn't get around to sending you a post card."

"Thanks," said Toby, stiffly in spite of himself. He couldn't forget that Windy Foot and he had beaten Jimmy and Whistle Stop in the race at the Webster County Fair. Jimmy had ridden to win the ten-dollar prize so that he could help his father on his farm and try to put something ahead toward agricultural college. He liked Jimmy. "Darn it," he said crossly, "I wish he could have come." Then he was ashamed of himself for his tone of voice. "Hey, Tish, how's Billy Blue?"

She gave a low giggle. "Billy said to tell you to your face that he'd have come along, but somebody has to keep an eye on the horses and that you knew cat's well he wouldn't let anybody else do it."

Toby roared. "Ho! He told me for cat's sake to get riding and stop talking. How are the horses? How's Golden Hind?"

"Beautiful," said Tish with a sigh. "And can she run!"

"I'll say," said Toby fervently. "How's Jigs?"

"Slow but still Jigs. How's Windy?"

"Fast," said Toby, trying to sound modest and not making it. "Even with a new sleigh—I mean, an old sleigh cut down. You wait till you see him." He was bragging. "Windy kind of pokes, Tish, because he isn't used to a slab-sided sleigh."

She grinned at him. "How's Matilda?"

"The best taken care of doll in the state."

"Huh," said Tish. "Then I was right."

"What about?"

"Never you mind." She looked off toward the hills. "You'll know what I mean when the time comes. I don't dast tell you what I've got for Betts because you'd tell her before tomorrow."

"I won't either!" said Toby indignantly. "Girls! You have more foxy ideas than a fox has burrows."

Tish laughed. "We certainly do. And what you don't know you won't worry about. How's your mother?"

"Swell, thanks," he said.

Then they rounded the butternut curve and came in sight of the farm.

She sat forward. "Is that Johnny I see?"

"That's Johnny. I told you he'd be whooping around."

Johnny waved so violently that he sat down in a drift. He flung snow right and left and struggled up. When Toby helped Tish down from the sleigh, the little boy threw himself into her arms, getting her plastered with whiteness. "Hello, Tish!"

"Hello, Johnny." Tish hugged him. "It's good to see you."

"I should think so," said Johnny, nuzzling against her cheek. "Here I've been waiting to see you all these years since the Fair!"

"Months," said Toby, picking up the suitcases.

"It felt like years," said Johnny stubbornly.

"It did," said Tish. "Hello, Betts."

Betsy clung to her, too. "H-hello, Tish," she stammered with excitement. "C-come on home!"

Mom was waiting, smiling in the doorway. "Merry Christmas, Jerry! Merry Christmas, Tish!" She shook hands with Jerry and kissed Tish. "My goodness, I'm glad you could get here! Come in!"

The kitchen was warm and smelled of new bread and pies and gingerbread and birchwood. "Where do you want me to put these suitcases, Mom?"

"Put Mr. Burnham's in the spare room. And you double up with Johnny so that Tish can have your room, because yours is bigger. Oh, and Toby, a couple of packages came for you. I put them in your closet."

"Thanks, Mom!" He struggled upstairs with the suitcases. They were heavy. At the top landing he recalled that he didn't know which was which and shouted down, "Hey, Tish!"

She came to the foot of the stairs with Betts and Johnny holding onto her hands. "What is it, Toby?"

"Which suitcase is yours?"

"The black one. Need any help?"

"No, thanks, not right this minute. But I'm going to, this afternoon." He winked elaborately toward the kids.

"Toby is up to no good," said Johnny, tugging at her right hand. "He's got something up his sleeve."

Toby hustled to put the two bags in the two rooms and returned to the head of the stairs in time to see Betts giving him the family signal of the left hand on the head and pointing with the right at Johnny.

Tish was leaning down. "Johnny, Toby tells me you can slide down the banister all by yourself. Let's see you."

"Oh!" cried Johnny, delighted. "You bet I can! You watch!" He scuttled up the stairs. "Toby, please lift me up."

Toby balanced him on the banister. "Have a nice bump," he said and let his little brother go.

Halfway down, Johnny slid dangerously toward the outer edge of the rail and Toby caught his breath and started to rush down the stairs, but Tish stood at the bottom, calling firmly, "Come on down, Johnny. We're here."

"I'm coming!" yelped Johnny, righting himself and landing hard against the newel post. "See?" he asked triumphantly. "I can slide like a star, can't I?"

Toby lifted him down. "You certainly can. Now give Tish a breath to wash her face."

"If I may," said Tish, trying hard not to laugh.

"Of course you may," said Johnny, seizing Betsy's hand and dragging her backward. "If you like that sort of thing. I don't."

"I should say you don't," said Betts, letting herself be dragged. "You're always grimy."

"I am not either so grimy! I'm just friendly to—to the ground and things."

"All right," said Betts. "Let's go see what Mom is up to."

Toby showed Tish where the bathroom was and where his room was. "I've got to fix some gifts. Come on in when you want to."

He hauled the catalogue presents from his closet, tore the coverings off, and chunked down on his heels to examine everything. Whew! Thank heavens the packages had come in time. He shook hands with himself and with the mail-order company in his mind and suddenly sat down on the floor. Now how in the world was he going to wrap up the doll carriage in tissue paper? It was an awkward shape to tie paper around. He was squatting on his heels, wheeling it up and down with one hand, trying to figure the problem out, when there was a gentle knock at his open door. He jumped.

"It's me. It's Tish."

"Come in, Tish. And please close the door in case the kids start peeking. How am I going to wrap this thing up?"

"Oh! A carriage! She'll love it, Toby!" For a second Tish looked as if she were going to cry.

"Huh?" he said brusquely. "What'll I do with it?"

"Don't wrap it up. Just tie it with ribbons and put it under the tree. She'll know it's for her when she sees it. When do you open your presents?"

"Christmas morning before breakfast. After milking. Maybe I could manage to put it under the tree at the last minute."

"I could get Betsy out of the living room somehow perhaps while you do."

"Will you try?"

"To-by!" It was Betsy calling. "Din-ner!"

"Co-ming!" Quickly he put the carriage and the other gifts back in his closet and closed the door. "Will you help me wrap things up when the kids have their naps after dinner?"

"Of course. And then may I see Windy Foot?"

"You bet!"

For once he walked sedately down the stairs beside Tish instead of flinging himself over the banister and zooming down.

"Tish, sit beside me!" clamored Johnny.

"Beside me," said Betts.

"Between the two of you," said Mom firmly. "Where in the world is Cliff?"

Dad looked worried. "Oh, around somewhere."

Just then Cliff came bursting in and said, "Jim, that barnacled bear!"

off the hills until we catch him or know which way he's gone."

"Where are you going?" Mom's face was pure white this time.

"After him," said Dad.

"But, Dad, how are we going to ski?" Toby asked anxiously. "Tish brought her skis and everything—"

"Wait till we find where he is," said Dad. "I don't think you'd enjoy being mauled."

Toby suddenly realized that this was important, more important than skiing. "Dad! Hey, Dad! May I go with you? I can help trail him!"

"No," said Dad with finality. "You've got to stay here and take care of the farm. He's apt to circle back this way."

"Aw," said Toby, disappointment making his voice wobble. "How can I shoot a bear with a BB gun?"

"You can't," said Dad. "But you rather remember, I think, that I taught you to shoot with the old Winchester, which has only two loads?"

"Yes, sir."

"Well, then," said Dad calmly, "you have two shots and don't waste them."

Toby grinned. "Don't worry, Dad."

"I'd better not have to," said Dad.

Toby perked up. "Boy, I hope that bear comes back!"

"Well, I don't," said Mom. "There's enough excitement around here without bears for Christmas. I wouldn't mind a cub, but a big one is too much of a good thing."

Dad chortled. "I can just see you feeding a cub from a baby's bottle. Mom, you're an easy mark for young ones, no matter what kind."

"Well," said Mom, her eyes flashing, "it's a good thing I am, if you ask me. Children come in all sizes, even six feet tall!"

Toby roared and choked. She meant Dad, of course. Dad came around the table and ruffled her hair.

"Get on with you," said Mom, her cheeks pink.

Betsy started to thump Toby and all of a sudden Toby wasn't choking. "Excuse me, Mom."

From the kitchen window he watched Dad and Cliff and Jerry climbing the south hill on snowshoes, shotguns under their arms. He stroked the double-barreled old Winchester, feeling grown up and very important. He was the man on the farm now, ready to defend his family and the stock against ten bears if necessary.

Mom sent Johnny and Betsy upstairs for naps. When Tish had finished helping with the dishes, she helped Toby wrap his gifts and he hid them in the closet once more. They went out to the stable to see Windy Foot, then returned to the house and played Chinese checkers. Every half hour Toby took the gun and circled the house and the barn, the pigpen, the stable, and the wagon shed. There was no sign of bear except the big tracks that Cliff had pointed out to him. The tracks were deep in the glittering crust of the sunlit snow on the west hayfield; they turned away from the barn near the silo and went loping off toward the south hill. For all his tenseness and excitement, Toby felt a chill down the back of his neck whenever he turned a corner of a building. He kept the gun ready.

Tish was as nervous as he was. She wanted to go with him on his rounds, but he wouldn't let her. They both made silly mistakes in the checker games and kept looking out of the living-room windows.

When he went out to the kitchen for a drink of water, he found Mom anxiously scanning the south hill. "I wish they'd come home," she said over her shoulder. "It'll begin to get dark in another hour. Poke, stop chewing those geranium leaves." She sighed and sat down in the rocker by the window and picked up her knitting. "There's a plate of fudge on the pantry shelf, Toby. I was just going to take it in to you."

"Thanks, Mom. And don't worry—they'll be home before dark."

"They didn't take flashlights and I forgot to remind them. Give a man a chance to go hunting something and he'll forget his own head. Not that I'm much better," she added with a wry grin.

Beside the wood box Ribs thumped his tail hope-fully for fudge and Toby gave him a piece. "Isn't it time the kids woke up?"

"Let them sleep," said Mom. "They'll be up late

tonight at the carol singing. The next time you go out, you'd better take a look at Georgette and see that she has plenty of hay. Or I'll go out myself."

"No, Mom! You stay in the house! I'll check on her."

"I've got to feed the chickens anyway."

"I'll feed 'em."

"It's been years since bears have been seen around this part of the state." She gazed out of the window again. "I phoned Bill Westover some time ago while you were out and told him the men had gone trailing. He said everybody thinks the bear must have come down from Canada because of the severe winter up there and the lack of food in the woods. Well, I wish he'd go right straight back to Canada and stay there." Mom knitted so violently that she dropped a stitch and said, "Drat!"

Toby grinned at her. "Mom, you stop having fidgets."

"All right," said Mom, scowling at her knitting. "You go eat fudge and let me fidget in peace."

7
Black Bear, White Dusk

WHEN Toby tramped outdoors the next time, the sun was slipping down behind the black pines on the western ridge and the sky was beginning to turn the cold apple green of a winter sunset. He fed the chickens, locked the hen-house door securely, and hurried toward the barn to check on Georgette. Leaning the gun carefully against the grain bin, he lit a lantern and hung it on a beam. The light threw strange shadows down the dim barn. The cattle were lowing restlessly. In the calving pen, Georgette looked up at him sadly from where she lay in the clean straw. He gave her some more hay, stroked her head, patted her shoulder.

From the stable he could hear the horses stamping and Windy Foot neighed nervously. He, too, wished that Dad would come home. He was beginning to be frightened. What if something had happened to Dad and Cliff and Jerry? What if they'd run into the bear and the bear had hurt them? He swallowed. He'd leave the lantern lit so that the men could see the glow from the barn windows.

Could bears climb through windows? He didn't know for sure, but if they could climb trees, he supposed they could reach windows, too. He thought of the windows in the tack room. Were they locked? But a bear could break glass with one swipe of a paw. He had just pulled the barn door shut and padlocked it when he heard Windy scream. Then there came a thunder of kicking hoofs. Toby's hair stood on end under his knitted cap.

The stable doors were locked. He'd seen to that before. He flicked the safety catch forward on the Winchester and slipped around the stable. The tack-room windows were whole. Windy and the horses were plunging and neighing in their stalls. Up in the house, Ribs was barking wildly. The cows bawled, the bull bellowed, the chickens were in pandemonium. And behind the barn in the pigpen, Florinda, the sow, and Frederick, her husband, were yelling like fiends.

Toby's skin was like ice and for a second the gun shook in his hands. Then he got mad. As he eased around the corner of the stable he saw an enormous black shape through the white dusk, reared on great hind feet, tugging at the back door of the stable. The padlock held. The bear growled with fury, backed up, and it looked to Toby as if he were going to rush the door.

"Windy!" Toby breathed and at the same instant fired toward the huge black chest.

The bear roared, swung his head to and fro, and

Toby fired toward the huge black chest.

dropped on all fours. Toby let go with the other, his last barrel, flung the gun away, and streaked for the house. In his panic he stumbled over a rock and fell flat. With snow in his mouth and eyes, he heard another shot and tried to burrow into the cold white earth. He couldn't breathe and he felt a clutch on his shoulder. He knew he was dead.

Something pulled him from the snow, shook him until he got the snow out of his mouth, and then hugged him. He gasped. But it wasn't the bear. It was Dad.

"Toby! You all right, boy?"

He couldn't speak yet. He grabbed Dad around the neck and hung on, still quaking with terror.

Dad patted him on the back. "Hold on, partner. It's all right. It's all right."

Cliff and Jerry came stumbling up.

"Barnacles on a bulrush!" said Cliff hoarsely. "Are you a good shot, kid!"

"You certainly are," said Jerry Burnham enthusiastically. "Got that big brute with both shots—right in the chest!"

Toby lifted his head from Dad's shoulder. "I—I did?"

"You bet!" said Dad, helping him to his feet.

"How'd you get here?" Toby asked, trying to stop his knees from banging together.

"We were following his tracks back down when we

heard the racket all over the place and we didn't waste any time."

"Wan't any grass growing under our feet," said Cliff. "Your Dad hit him in the back when he was chasing you, but he toppled the next minute from your two shots in his front."

"What's the matter with your legs, Toby?" Dad asked, leaning down. "Come on, we'd better get you into the house."

"N-nothing," Toby said. "I guess I skinned my shin on the rock, that's all." He limped along beside Dad. Dad kept his arm around his shoulders.

"Jerry, take my gun in the house, will you?" Cliff asked. "I'll go quiet the horses and start milking."

"Sure thing, Cliff."

Before they reached the woodshed door Dad said, his arm tightening, "I'm mighty proud of you, Toby."

Toby's teeth were still chattering. He stammered, "Th-thanks, D-Dad."

Mom had heard them coming and she was standing in the open kitchen door with a flashlight, the kids clustered around her. "Jim! Toby! Are you all right?"

"Jerry!" cried Tish, looking white and shaken.

"You've got a hero for a son, Mary," said Dad, and Mom put her arms around both of them. "Hey, get that flashlight out of my back! He killed that critter all by himself!"

"I don't care what he killed as long as you're all here," said Mom, her voice uneven. "Where's Cliff?"

"Out in the barn. I got to go help him milk. Do something about Toby's leg. See you later."

Jerry put the guns in the gun rack near the woodshed door. Then he turned and grinned at Tish. "Hello," he said and kissed her cheek.

"Oh, Jerry!" said Tish, seizing his arm with both hands. Suddenly she burst into tears and tore out of the kitchen and up the stairs.

Jerry gazed after her. "Well, I'll be—" he said with amazement. "She never did that before."

Betsy and Johnny were frantic with excitement. They helped Toby get his Mackinaw off, both of them tugging at the sleeves. Johnny pulled off his boots, Betsy took off his heavy socks. Mom glanced at his lacerated shin and went for a basin of warm water.

"I can do that, Mom," he protested.

"All right. Betts, get the iodine."

The warmth of the kitchen, the warmth of their affection felt fine. But he didn't hanker to meet any more bears right away.

8
Christmas Eve

AFTER supper they all went into the living room. Toby turned the baseboard switch and the small colored lights blossomed on the tree. They gazed at the lovely spruce with its softly gleaming gold and silver and red and blue and green balls, its loops of white popcorn, its gay little bunches of partridge berries.

They contemplated the tree in silence for a few minutes until Johnny began to sing "Santa Claus Is Coming to Town," leaning against Jerry Burnham's chair.

"Come on, everybody," said Dad. "We'd better get started for the village and the carol singing. Bundle up good and warm—the temperature's going down."

Toby put the fire screen carefully in place, took one last look at the tree, and switched off the lights.

It was a beautiful evening, clear and cold, and the sky was washed by a surf of brilliant stars. Mom rode in the front of the truck between Dad and Jerry Burnham. Deep in the clean straw in the rear of the truck, Toby sat across from Tish who, flanked by Betsy and

Johnny, kept tucking the horse blankets around them. As fast as she tucked them, one or the other bounced up to career against her and ask questions.

Johnny asked abruptly, "Where's Cliff? Toby, we forgot Cliff! Tell Dad to turn around!"

"Cliff stayed home on purpose."

"On purpose why?" Johnny plunged across the truck and landed against Toby's sore leg.

"Ouch! Sit down."

"I am," said Johnny meekly, crawling into Toby's lap. "Did I hurt you, Toby?"

"Yes. Now stay still for a minute, will you? Cliff didn't want to come, that's all." Toby didn't want to mention Georgette's calf. "He says he can't sing anyway, so what's the use of his coming to the carols?"

"Cliff can, too, sing!" exclaimed Johnny indignantly. "He was singing day before yesterday. Tish, how long can you stay?"

Toby leaned forward. "How long, Tish?"

"I don't know for sure," she replied slowly. "It depends on Jerry. He thought we'd better leave the day after Christmas."

"Oh, no!" cried Toby and Betts and Johnny all together.

Toby surveyed Tish's face, unsmiling under the stars and in the reflected light from the white hills. She looked back at him gravely. "Tish, can't you stay till New Year's?"

"I wish we could. But we're farmers, too. And we

have to be there, even if Ed, our hired man, and Billy Blue are taking care of the cows and the horses. You know how it is, Toby."

"Yes," he answered gruffly. "I know. But I wish—gosh, we won't have time to ski and skate and do half the things—"

When they passed the first street lamps on the outskirts of the village, Dad had to slow down. Cars and sleighs and pungs were entering the main road from the side roads that wound up into the hills. Shouts and laughter drifted through the village as Dad parked on the west side of the square. Everybody piled out of the truck and hurried toward the crowd gathered in the packed-down snow near the bandstand.

The tree was so beautiful, rearing tall and gleaming into the clear blue evening, that Toby caught his breath. Johnny seized his hand and stood with his mouth open, for once not uttering a sound. Betsy and Tish gazed raptly at the colored lights. Mom and Dad and Jerry Burnham glanced from the children to the tree and smiled at one another.

It was cold but it wasn't too cold. Toby peered up at the shaking stars and sniffed the air. It would be clear tomorrow morning, but he bet himself that it would snow some time tomorrow afternoon. He could smell snow days and miles away. He grinned at Orion, turned and located the Dippers and Cassiopeia's Chair. One of these days, he promised himself, or rather, one of these nights, he'd have to give Betsy and Johnny a star lesson. And in the spring when it grew warm, they could take his star map outdoors and really study the sky. So far they'd only turned his planisphere around and around and stared at it and made no sense out of it whatever.

A golden note from a trumpet made everyone jump. There in the bandstand was part of the village band, trying to play their instruments with woolen gloves on. Miss Aldrich, the school music teacher, stood on the top step of the bandstand, her baton in her white-gloved hand, and started the carols. The voices of the villagers and the farmers rose joyfully around the tall tree.

> *O little town of Bethlehem,*
> *How still we see thee lie.*
> *Above thy deep and dreamless sleep*
> *The silent stars go by. . . .*

Toby caught Dad's and Mom's glance and they nodded at him without stopping their singing. Mom's eyes were bright and Dad closed his mouth for a moment to grin affectionately at Toby. Jerry Burnham was staring at the tree, not singing, and Toby saw with dismay that Tish wasn't singing either but was watching Jerry. Oh, gosh, he hoped that Tish and Jerry would be happy this Christmas. He swallowed a bump in his neck and missed a whole line. Gently he shoved Johnny toward Tish.

Johnny looked up. "What is it, Toby?"

"Hold onto Tish's hand so she won't feel lonesome."

"Sure," whispered Johnny. "But how can she feel lonesome when I'm here?"

"She can't," Toby whispered back, "if you hold her hand."

"Why don't you?"

"No, you!" said Toby hoarsely.

Warbling loudly, Johnny caught Tish's left mitten and swung arms.

Startled, Tish gave him a wavering smile and hummed with him.

It came up-oo-oon a mi-i-night clear, shouted Johnny. *That gl-l-or-us so-song of ole—*

Toby whooped into the rest of the carol. The voices of the crowd gathered strength and soared. Then they sang "Come All Ye Faithful" and "Good King Wenceslas" and "Jingle Bells." The men in the band kept taking off their woolen gloves between songs and blowing on their fingers and putting their gloves back on again. Their breathing was a brief white mist in the sharp air. The carols finished with "Silent Night."

Laughing and chattering, the crowd broke up and moved across the square toward the stores to do their last-minute shopping.

The Clarks and the Burnhams strolled slowly down the street toward the truck. In front of the drugstore, Dick Norton, who sat across the aisle from Toby in the seventh grade, was yelling, "Mistletoe for sale!

Mistletoe right here, straight from Montana! Mistle-toe, ten cents a spray! Mistle-toe!"

"Hey," said Toby, pausing. "Hi, Dick! Where'd you get it?"

"Uncle of mine sent it to us from Montana," answered Dick. "Want some?"

"Two sprays." Toby handed Dick a quarter.

Dick gave him back a nickel. "Thanks, Toby. Merry Christmas."

"You, too, Dick." He gave his friend a clap on the shoulder. "Why don't you come out and go skiing some day this week?"

"Will if I can. But I've got to help my father mend harness during vacation." He looked at Toby critically. "Say, what're you limping for?"

"Fell on a rock." He debated with himself. Should he tell Dick about the bear or would that be bragging? Before he decided, he heard himself saying casually, "Shot a black bear this afternoon."

"You what?" asked Dick, bursting into laughter. "Aw, go on, Toby! Quit telling whoppers."

"Okay," said Toby, his feelings hurt. Then he laughed with Dick. "Scared me so, I ran away and fell flat on my map. Ask my father. Come on out and ski if you can make it."

"You bet I will," said Dick. "Can I see the bear?"

"Sure thing. So long, Dick."

"So long, Superman," chuckled Dick. "Mistletoe! Mistletoe from Montana!"

Toby saw Dad go into the general store. He limped hurriedly after the rest of the family. "Mom! Here!"

"What is it, Toby?"

"Mistletoe. You hang it in the dining-room doorway so we can kiss you without having to catch you on the run between the stove and the pantry!"

"Toby Clark!" Mom laughed. "You're as full of mischief as your father!"

"I've got another spray for Windy Foot and I'm going to hang it over his head in his stall, and everybody will have to go out tomorrow and kiss his nose for Christmas!"

"Naturally," said Mom, her green eyes dancing. "We'd go out anyway to tell him Merry Christmas. I'm making some maple mousse for dessert, and he can have a large dish of it for his present."

"Oh, boy!" said Toby. "I bet he'll like that better than a strawberry ice-cream cone."

"I'll sit behind, on the way home, Mary," Jerry Burnham said. "You'll need room for Johnny."

"All right, Jerry." She settled the little boy on the front seat. "Tired, John Christopher Clark?" she asked.

Johnny sighed happily. "It was nice looking up in the tree, Mom. Stars winking in the sky, stars winking in my eye." He nuzzled against Mom's shoulder. "Good night," he said peacefully.

They had just settled in the back of the truck when Dad climbed into the front and started the engine.

"Told Bill Westover and Hank Higgins they won't have to worry about that bear any more, thanks to Toby. Home, Mrs. Clark?"

"Home, James," said Mom, and yelled back, "Everybody all set?"

"Race away!" shouted Jerry Burnham and put one arm around Betsy and the other around Tish.

Across the truck, Toby grinned at him and lifted his face to the wheeling stars.

When they reached the farm, there was a light in the barn. Dad told Mom, "I'll be in later, Mary," and after putting the truck in the wagon shed, he stalked toward the barnyard.

Toby carried Johnny, still asleep, into the house. Ribs barked a frantic welcome and Johnny promptly woke up and beamed around the kitchen.

"I had the wonderfulest dream!" he stated. "I thought it was Christmas."

"It is—tomorrow." Toby unfastened his snow suit. "It is—tomorrow."

Johnny balanced on one leg, yawned deeply. "Tomorrer?"

"Hop to bed," said Mom briskly. "All of you."

Upstairs Toby helped Johnny undress before he began to take off his own things. Johnny turned a somersault on the bed, jumped between the covers, and sang himself a lullaby. "Tomorrow's Christmas, yup, yup, yup! I wish tomorrow would hurry up. Tomorrow's Christmas, ha, ha, ha! And I've got to go to sleep, pshaw, pshaw, pshaw. Good night, Toby." He bounced over onto his stomach.

"Good *night*," mumbled Toby. He forced himself to stay awake until he was sure that Johnny was sound asleep. Then he slipped noiselessly out of bed, put on his blue bathrobe, and tiptoed out into the hall.

He had moved his gifts, this evening, from the closet in his room to the hall closet where Mom kept the household linen and the blankets. As he was cautiously taking his presents from the far corner of the closet, there was a squeak behind him and the door of his own room opened. Tish stood there in pajamas and a dark green dressing gown, her arms loaded with packages.

"Hello," he said softly and put his finger to his lips.

She smiled and nodded and went silently downstairs. He gathered up his gifts and followed her. The doll carriage would wait until the last minute in the morning.

Mom was placing small presents in the branches of the lighted tree; the larger ones she had piled on the floor beneath the lowest boughs. "Still awake?" Her leaf-brown hair was going every which way. "I'm putting Betsy's gifts on, too—she was too sleepy to do it herself. Ouch!" She caught a curl on a spruce twig and Toby laughed and unfastened it.

"What's the matter with this family, Mom? We seem to be getting all tangled up with bears or trees or something tonight. How's Georgette?"

"I don't know yet. The men are all out in the barn. Did you know, Tish, that Georgette is giving Betsy a Christmas present?"

"Yes, I did, Mrs. Clark. I mean, I knew she was having a calf but I didn't know it was for Betts." She placed her gifts under the tree and straightened. "Mrs. Clark, may I ask you something?"

"Why, of course, Tish. And I wish you'd call me Aunt Mary, if you want to."

Tish gulped. "T-that was just what I was going to ask you. If I might. If you'd mind."

"Come here, Tish," said Mom quietly. She put her arms around Tish and kissed her cheek. "Now you sleep tight like a fine girl. Tomorrow's going to be a big day."

Tish hugged Mom. "Good night, Aunt Mary." She bolted for the stairway.

"Gosh, Mom!" said Toby.

"Hop!" said Mom in a funny voice. "The idea of your being up at this hour!"

"Oh, Mom! That was just what she needed! How'd you know?"

Mom gazed at him and he felt knee-high. Then her green eyes twinkled. She gave him a light spank. "Tobias Clark—to bed!"

He scooted for the stairs.

9

Christmas Morning

WHEN Toby awoke on Christmas morning, he sat up and hugged his knees. He discovered he'd pulled the covers off Johnny, who was dreaming on his stomach, and tucked his little brother in again. It was still dark but there was a wonderful air of anticipation through the house. He heard it in the muffled sounds from downstairs and he smelled it in the aroma of fresh coffee and the odor of evergreens, and he sat still, savoring it. He looked out of Johnny's window and saw stars different from those he saw from his own room.

His shin still hurt but not enough to keep him from going skiing today. He eased out of bed so as not to awaken Johnny, dressed, and skipped washing. He had to get Betsy's carriage downstairs before she woke up.

He stowed it in the coat closet under the stairs and hurried toward the kitchen. He was late for milking.

Mom was busy in the pantry. She turned and patted his shoulder and exclaimed, "Oh, goodness, I've got you all flour! Merry Christmas, Tobias!"

"Merry Christmas, Mom!" He brushed the hair out of his eyes.

"Haven't you combed your hair yet?"

"Didn't stop to. Will later. I'll fill the wood box now so I won't have to bother after milking."

"Good. And light the tree, will you, Toby? Everybody still asleep?"

"Johnny and Betts are, anyway. Dunno about the Burnhams. Gosh, that coffee smells good!"

"My fine bottomless pit," said Mom, looking abstracted.

He turned on the lights and admired the shining tree laden with gifts. He backed up and wished he could draw the tree and all the family love it held. Darn it, someday he would, he promised himself.

"Mom!" he called, making his voice imperative and frantic.

"What is it?" She rushed to the dining-room doorway.

He laughed, made a dive for her, and on tiptoe kissed her under the mistletoe.

"Toby Clark, you imp! I'd forgotten all about that bulrush."

"Fooled you, Mom!"

"Skedaddle," said Mom with mock ferocity, her green eyes steady. "Go help Dad."

When he burst out of the woodshed door, he could almost smell spring. But the hills were white with their green-black climbing boughs laden with snow, marching toward the sky. Beneath the layers of snow, he knew, were young pines and young spruce and young maples sleeping, waiting for the March thaw. He rattled his Mackinaw pocket of sugar lumps and avoided looking toward the corner of the stable where the rock was and behind that, where the bear still lay like a black sprawled dreadfulness, drifted over a little by the wind-blown snow. He tried not to look, but he couldn't help seeing the bear out of the corner of his eye. He didn't feel proud at all. He simply felt sorry for the bear. And he felt sorry for himself because he'd had to shoot the bear. But if he hadn't, the bear would have shoved the stable door down, and Windy—

As if the pony knew what he was thinking, Windy whinnied loudly and Toby whistled and Windy did a tattoo on his stall floor.

"Hold on," said Toby and gave each of the other horses an apple for Christmas-breakfast dessert. Windy whooshed and stamped impatiently.

Toby flung his arms around the pony's neck. "Hello, Windy! Hello, boy!"

Windy nuzzled his hair and pranced.

"You want your apple now or after breakfast?"

Windy replied that he'd like it immediately, thank you. While he was munching the apple, Toby climbed up on the manger and fastened the mistletoe on the beam over Windy's head, slid down and kissed the wondering pony on the nose. "That's for Christmas. So's this." He opened a package he'd hidden in the tack room and presented Windy with a red jockey cap. He'd cut two holes in the top for Windy's ears, but when he put it on, the pony shook his head violently from side to side and up and down and looked at Toby with a dubious eye.

"Hold still," Toby said, having to laugh. "If Tillie and Tossie can wear horse hats with geraniums and daisies, I guess you can wear a riding cap. Oh, Windy, you look funny! All right, hold still, boy, while I fix it so it's more comfortable."

Windy asked what in thunder was the idea anyhow.

Toby dug a lump of sugar from his Mackinaw pocket and Windy was somewhat pacified. He was still shaking his head when Toby closed the stable door. "Easy does it, Windy. You'll be used to it in no time."

What next? asked Windy with an indignant whicker.

When he entered the barn Toby sniffed the warm hay-scented breath of the cattle, and the cows turned their heads in their stanchions to observe him with soft dark eyes. He stamped the snow from his boots on the plank floor and went down the barn, searching for Dad.

"Hello, Toby." Dad was leaning his forehead against Hepzibah's tan satin flank. The milk struck noisily against the side of the galvanized pail.

"Dad! Merry Christmas!"

"Same to you, son." Dad grinned at him. "Go see what Georgette's got for Betts."

"Golly, Dad, did you get any sleep?"

Dad kept on milking Hepzibah. "Who wants to sleep at a time like this?"

"Barnacles on a bulrush!" said Cliff's rough voice behind him. "Don't tell me you waked up."

"Cliff, you know I always wake up."

"Yup," said Cliff morosely, setting down his full pail and hunting through his overalls for a stick of wintergreen chewing gum. "When you *think* of it, you wake up. How you're ever going to be a farmer beats me."

"I am, though, and I'm going to be an artist at the same time!" Toby told him fiercely.

Cliff shook his grizzled head sadly. "Have a stick of gum? Happy New Year."

LEE TOWNSEND

Toby went down the barn, searching for Dad.

"Thanks, Cliff. You, too. I've got to go see Georgette."

Cliff picked up his pail and started toward the big milk cans. "Smartest thing in the world. For a cow. That Georgette," he said proudly.

Toby dashed for the calving pen on the far side of the barn. He unfastened the hook and opened the whitewashed gate. "Oh, Georgette!" She looked up at him peacefully, gave a low moo, and returned to chewing her cud.

Against her side lay a long-legged dark-gold calf. Toby dropped to his knees in the straw and put out a hand to stroke the baby's hard little head. But the calf, astonished and startled, struggled to its feet, stood wobbling with its forelegs going in opposite directions and its knees turned in. It blatted loudly. The effort of bawling was too much for it: it capsized into the straw and Georgette moved her head and washed it into safety again. But the baby gazed at Toby with great innocent, puzzled eyes, and very gently he smoothed the golden hide and murmured, "It's all right. You're here. It's all right."

"To-by!" Dad's voice bounced against the rafters of the barn.

He called, "Right, Dad," and stood up as quietly as possible so as not to disturb the calf again. He went around to the other side of the cow and patted her shoulder. "Georgette."

"Moo," said Georgette without much energy.

"Good girl," said Toby, and fastened the pen gate behind him.

When milking was over Dad said, "Toby, you and Cliff go on up to the house. When everybody's ready in the living room, you sneak out the back door and whistle Windy's signal and I'll bring the calf in. Tell Mom."

"Sure, Dad." He jogged along beside Cliff, happiness bouncing in his chest. He and Cliff washed at the kitchen sink, nodded at each other.

"All ready?" Mom asked, rushing into the kitchen. Her cheeks were pink and her hair was curling every which way and she looked as excited and young as Toby felt.

"Hey, Mom." He explained about Dad's waiting for the whistle signal.

Mom nodded and yanked open the oven door. "Those turkeys," she said, basting away. "I'll be there in a minute."

In the living room Betsy and Johnny were sitting beside Jerry Burnham on the davenport, each holding one of his hands, their faces shining with soap and water and anticipation.

Tish was leaning on the back of a chair. She caught his eye and gave him a ghost of a wink. She was wearing a white woolen shirt and dark green slacks and had a white ribbon in her hair. Toby winked back and gave a slight nod toward Betsy.

Tish began to cough and put her hand over her

mouth. "Oh, excuse me," she said. "I seem to have a tickle in my throat. Betsy, would you mind showing me where the cold milk is? I think if I had a—I think if I had a small glass, it would stop this choking."

Betts was off the davenport at once. "I'll get you some, Tish!"

"No, come and show me where it is, please." She took Betsy's hand and they hustled into the dining room with Tish coughing valiantly all the way. Toby chuckled and Mom nodded. He went hastily to the hall closet, pulled out the doll carriage, and placed it behind the tree so that it was completely hidden by the low back boughs. "Maybe she won't notice it right away," he whispered loudly.

"Hey!" Johnny said.

"Hush for once, Johnny," Mom said. "Toby, you'd better whistle for Dad now. We can't start till he gets here to play Santa Claus."

At the woodshed door Toby gave the three-whistle signal. Windy neighed frantically in his stall and his hoofs beat a wild tattoo on the floor. Toby yelled, "Easy, Windy." Dad came across the barnyard with Georgette's baby in his arms. Toby held the woodshed door and the kitchen door open for him and tagged behind him into the living room.

There was immediate bedlam. Johnny shrieked with delight, Mom and Jerry Burnham laughed, Cliff muttered, "Huh!" and Tish cried, "Oh, the darling!" Betsy jumped up and down and shouted, "Dad! Dad, where'd you get it?"

Trying desperately to keep his face straight and not to look as if he had swallowed the sun, Dad crouched and stood the quivering calf on the rag rug, holding it up. "Betsy," he said, "come here."

She went slowly to him and stretched out a shaking hand toward the calf's nose. Her eyes were as dark as the small creature's.

"It's yours," said Dad. "It's my present and Georgette's. Merry Christmas, Betsy."

"Mine?" Betsy's voice was so faint that Toby could scarcely hear her. "Me?"

"Yours," said Dad. "What are you going to name it?"

Betsy looked dazed. "You mean for keeps?"

"For keeps."

"Oh!" Her lips trembled. "Thank you." She touched the calf's nose. "Angelina," she gulped.

Cliff made a strange sound. Betts looked up at him. "Well," said Cliff, clearing his throat, "don't see how as you can call it Angelina. It's a boy calf."

Betsy and the calf gazed at each other. "Kris," said Betts. "After Kris Kringle."

"Fine," said Mom.

"I better take Kris back to the barn," said Cliff hastily. "His mother'll be worried about him. You folks go ahead with the presents—I'll be right back." He bent and scooped the calf up in his arms.

"I'll be out to see you later, Kris!" promised Betsy, her eyes following Cliff. "Oh, Dad!" She flung herself into his arms.

"Hey," said Dad. "You can't cry on Christmas."

"I'm not crying! I'm—"

"Of course you aren't," he reassured her. "Now blow your nose and let's see what's here for everybody." He stood up. "Where'll I start, Mom?"

"Anywhere," answered Mom cheerfully. "The branches first, I guess. Or wherever."

"Here we go," said Dad. One by one he took the presents from the tree and read the gift cards aloud. The living room became a gay confusion of voices, assisted wholeheartedly by Ribs, who barked and pranced wildly from one person to another, and by Poke, who kept batting the tissue paper tossed on the floor and getting herself half strangled in red and green and blue and silver-spangled ribbon.

Johnny blasted away feverishly on a mouth organ from Tish while he shoved across the rug on small skis from Dad.

Toby felt his face grow hot while Jerry Burnham unwrapped the gray-framed portrait of the racing mare, Golden Hind. Jerry held the drawing off and studied it. "By Jove, Toby, this is excellent! I didn't know you could draw this well."

"I'm glad you like it, Mr. Burnham," Toby stammered.

Cliff gave Ribs a brown leather collar with a name

plate. Toby fastened the collar around the puppy's neck and Ribs promptly sat down and scratched at it violently. Everybody laughed at him, and he retreated behind Cliff's chair and flopped on his stomach, his nose on his paws, his dark eyes mournfully protesting. Cliff reached around and rubbed his ears and his tail thumped feebly. "He'll get used to it by tonight," Cliff said.

Tish watched her father as he opened her gift to him—a beautifully illustrated book on race horses. He looked up at her and she kissed the top of his head. "Merry Christmas, Jerry."

Dad was holding a package out. "Toby—from Mom."

"Oh, Mom!" It was a box of pastels, together with a block of pastel drawing paper and a bottle of fixative with a blower. "Gosh, Mom, how did you know I wanted pastels?"

"I didn't think you'd want to do just pen and pencil and chalk drawings if you're going to enter things in the Fair exhibit in the fall."

Toby cantered over and put his arms around her. "Thanks, Mom!"

"My goodness, Toby, you've mussed up my hair!"

"I have not, and besides it looks great mussed!"

Dad poked around in back of the tree. "What's this?" he asked loudly and wheeled the doll carriage out.

Betsy squealed and rushed for the carriage. "Ma-

tilda! It's for Matilda! Oh, wait till I go get her!" She
tore out of the room and up the stairs.

Toby and Tish grinned at each other.

Dad tossed Toby's catnip mouse to Poke who
sniffed it and at once appeared to lose her mind. Her
black tail lashing, she batted it furiously, chased it,
rolled on it. Sitting back on her haunches, she caught
it in her front paws and tossed it up in the air, doing
wonderful contortions, chased it again, rumbling
wildly in her throat. Ribs watched her with astonish-
ment for a minute, arose and went to investigate, but
Poke humped and spat at him, and when he retreated
to Cliff's chair, she skidded the catnip mouse across
the floor toward the dining room.

Betsy returned with Matilda and placed her tenderly
in the doll carriage, covering her with a blue bath
towel for a blanket.

"I'll make you a patchwork quilt for her," Mom
promised.

"Couldn't I knit her a blanket, Mom? Straight
knitting like Toby's muffler?"

"I don't see why not," smiled Mom.

"To Cliff from Johnny," announced Dad.

"Barnacles!" said Cliff. "Green ear muffs!" He fastened them on his head. "Ain't I the handsome one?"

The family agreed that he was, laughing at him as
he cocked his head from one side to the other, trying
to look hoity-toity.

"Where's Poke?" asked Dad. "She has a present from Cliff."

"I'll go get her," Johnny offered and scuttled toward the kitchen. He returned with the cat upside down in his arms.

"Here you are, Poke." Dad fastened a small scarlet collar with a shiny bell around her neck.

Poke tried to wriggle her head out of the collar, didn't succeed, and flew in a fury back toward the kitchen.

"Tish!"

"Jodhpurs!" she exclaimed. "Thank you, Jerry!" She held the brown whipcord pants up to her waist and admired them.

"I'll get you some boots for your birthday," Jerry told her. "Then you'll be all set for training next spring."

"When *is* your birthday?" Toby asked.

"March seventeenth," she laughed. "Saint Patrick's day."

"Toby—from me," said Dad with a grin.

He could tell it was a book and he tore off the paper excitedly. And what a book! It was a big collection of the lives of famous artists, with colored illustrations of their work. He gulped, "Boy, oh, boy, Dad! This is something!"

Johnny had a pup tent, an Indian suit, an alphabet book, and a knapsack. He was very busy being a musical Indian chief.

Toby watched Mom anxiously as she took the tissue paper from the birch-log candlestick with its three red candles.

"Did you make this, Toby?"

He nodded, fidgeting.

"It'll be lovely in the center of the table. We'll light it for dinner."

He sighed, feeling pleased with himself.

"Tish," said Dad, making a low bow.

Laughing, she bowed back. It was a book like Toby's, only this time it was the lives of famous doctors, and she said, "Mr. Clark, it's marvelous!"

"Mary," said Dad.

"Yes, Jim?"

"From your loving husband," said Dad and kissed Mom's nose.

She opened the large box with hurried fingers and gasped as she lifted out a soft green chenille housecoat that matched her eyes, and a pair of leather slippers in a darker green for contrast. "Jim Clark!"

"Put 'em on," ordered Dad. He gazed at her with admiration. "Best looking girl in Webster County, not to mention the state!" The family agreed with him enthusiastically. Mom blushed and her eyes became greener and brighter and her brown leaf-curly hair seemed to curl more than ever.

Toby smiled at her. "You look beautiful, Mom!"

"Don't flatter me," she said, laughing, "or I'll never put on a kitchen apron again!"

"To me from Cliff," growled Dad, and he produced
a black leather belt with an initialed silver buckle.
"Cliff, you old rascal!"

"Aw," said Cliff, scratching his right ear with embar-
rassment and getting his ear muffs crooked.

"Here, Ribs!" Dad whistled and tossed the puppy
the hard-rubber bone from Toby.

Ribs seized the bone and retreated with it behind
Cliff's chair where he gnawed it happily, trying to
sound ferocious.

Tish was delighted with the drawing of Jigs. "This
is grand, Toby. It looks just like her."

He flushed. "Gosh, I hope so."

"Betsy," called Dad. "Come here. From Tish."

She deserted the doll carriage and came running.
In a red Christmas box covered with holly lay a doll's
outfit: a winter coat and a dress, made of maroon
wool and trimmed with gray astrakhan, and a gay little
round astrakhan hat.

"Oh! For Matilda! Help me dress her up, Tish!"

"Of course, Betts. I hope they fit. I made them out
of a dress of mine that I'd outgrown."

They did fit. "Lookit!" demanded Betts. "Lookit
Matilda! Isn't she—isn't she—" She had no words to
describe the wonder of her child.

"She sure as woodchucks is," agreed Cliff, taking
his ear muffs off. "These things kind of itch in the
house," he said apologetically.

"You'll get chilblains if you wear them in the house," Johnny told him severely.

Cliff chuckled and unscrewed and screwed back his nest of screw drivers over and over, like a boy with a new toy.

"Tish, did you make these, too?" Mom sniffed the lavender and orrisroot sachet packets tied with narrow blue and pink and yellow and green and red and purple ribbons. "They smell like an old-fashioned garden."

Tish nodded. "I have an herb patch in my garden at home."

"Poke," called Dad. "Kitty, kitty! Here, puss, puss!"

Poke came jingling with her tail high. "Merow?" she asked and gave her collar a whack.

Dad bounced a red ball on a rubber string in front of her whiskers. "Betsy gave you this."

Poke batted at the ball, chasing it to and fro as it swung.

"Let's hitch it on the doorknob," Toby suggested.

"The kitchen doorknob," said Mom.

When he came back from the kitchen, Betts was putting Matilda into a white doll's bed that Jerry Burnham had given her. Johnny was lying on his stomach in the middle of a pile of tissue paper, frowning studiously at his alphabet book.

Dad handed Toby Tish's present. It was a palette for oil paints, and although he didn't have any oils, he promised himself that he would save his allowance and buy some as soon as possible. With learning how to use pastels and oils, this was going to be a fine year. "Gosh, Tish, thanks!"

"Toby—from Betsy."

He wondered what on earth it could be, because she had won it as a prize, the last day of school, for her story about a mouse. When he saw that it was a pedometer, he burst out laughing. "Betts! This is grand, but what are they giving girls pedometers as prizes for? Do they want you to walk and get thinner?"

"Nope," answered Betsy calmly, straightening Matilda's hat. "What I won was a book of Hiawatha, but we have it here at home anyway; so I swapped it with Neddy Tucker for the pedometer because he has a pedometer anyway and he wanted Hiawatha."

The family roared. "Betts, you'd make a first-rate horse trader," Dad told her. "Here's something from Johnny."

Mom tied the little blue ribbons on Betsy's pigtails.

"Now I match my sweater," Betts said and clasped Matilda to her chest. "And Matilda matches all over."

"Snakes!" exploded Cliff when he saw the fur-lined leather gloves. "I sure ain't going to freeze this winter! Much obliged, Jim."

"Toby—from Jerry Burnham."

He gaped at the punching bag and the boxing gloves. "Thanks, Mr. Burnham. Oh, boy!"

"Heard you were a pretty good boxer," Jerry said

with a slight grin, "and I thought you might want to keep in practice."

"I sure do!"

"What a lovely crazy Christmas!" said Mom happily. "I've got to go start the pancakes. Toby, you and Tish clear up in here, will you? Johnny and Betsy, get out of the way. I've got to take my housecoat off."

"Oh, no, Mom!" the children clamored. "Keep it on!"

"Keep it on, Mary," said Dad, kissing her cheek.

"While I'm cooking?" said Mom, taking it off and folding it carefully. "I should say not! I'd spatter it, and I'd burn everything just from looking at it and patting myself. You behave, Jim Clark, if you want any breakfast!"

The children giggled. It was Christmas, all right. It was the beginning of a beautiful day of nonsense and teasing and love and fun. Betsy returned to Matilda, Johnny returned to his alphabet, and Toby and Tish cleaned up. The living room was littered with bright paper and ribbon and stickers and tags and string. Poke came in and decided this crinkle of paper was all for her benefit and had to be shooed out. The room was back to normal finally.

They were looking at the books Dad had given them when Mom called from the dining room, "Yoo-hoo! Everybody!"

10
The Wishing Deer

WHEN breakfast was over, the Clark family and the Burnham family traipsed out to the stable and the barn to visit the animals.

After a heated argument, Johnny was persuaded to wear his snow suit over his Indian costume and to exchange his feathered headdress for his red toque. He tramped glumly after Toby, muttering to himself. But once in the stable, he became cheerful again and climbed on the mangers to pat the noses of Jake and Serena and Tillie and Tossie. He and Betsy gave each of the horses a lump of sugar, while Toby hurried to put Windy's scarlet jockey cap on properly for his Christmas company.

Johnny whooped at the mistletoe fastened on the beam over the Shetland's head. "Lift me up, Toby! I've got to kiss him!" He kissed Windy's nose and thrust a lump of sugar into his mouth at the same time. Windy lifted his head so quickly that he bopped Johnny's chin. "Ow! Bad Windy!"

[127]

Toby perched him on Windy's back. "He isn't bad. He didn't mean to bang you."

Johnny blinked rapidly and rubbed his chin. "He's got an awful hard head, Toby," he said sadly.

"Well, yours isn't exactly soft."

Cliff came out of the tack room. "Ready for Windy's presents?" he asked Dad.

"Sure, Cliff. Come on, Johnny, we need Windy's back." He lifted the little boy to the stable floor. "Here, Toby."

"Wow!" said Toby, gazing at the bright red pony blanket. He flung it over Windy's dappled hide. "Doesn't he look pretty special, Dad?"

"It matches his cap," Tish said.

Johnny warbled, patting the blanket, "Windy's got a nice red coat, Windy's got a nice red cap, Windy's

Tillie and Tossie

got such pretty ears, and I can sit on his nice spine lap!"

"Toby, this is for the sleigh." Mom handed him a red Hudson's Bay blanket with black stripes on each end. "It'll keep your knees warm when you and Betts are driving to school this winter."

"And you'll have a black bearskin robe later," Dad told him, waving his hand toward outdoors.

Cliff stalked jingling from the tack room. "This here's an old winter harness I cut down to fit him." The worn but polished black leather tinkled with small gleaming bells.

Toby took a deep breath. "Everybody thinks of everything, don't they?" he inquired happily.

"Your grammar's crooked," said Dad fondly. "But who cares on Christmas?"

Serena and Jake
LEE TOWNSEND

"Not me," stated Johnny airily.

"Obviously," said Mom. "You mean, *not I*."

"Do I?" asked Johnny, giving her a radiant smile.

"Tish, will you go sleighing with me this afternoon?" Toby gave the harness a shake to hear the bells.

"I'd love to, Toby."

The family and the Burnhams paraded hilariously through the barn, admiring the cows and Ira, the bull.

When they came to the calving pen, Betsy squeaked, "Oh, look at Georgette! Look at Kris! Cliff, did you do that?"

He shuffled his heavy boots and gazed fixedly toward the grain bin. "Ei-yup," he admitted. "They got just as much right to be decorated as anybody else."

Toby laughed. Georgette wore a spray of pine fastened to each of her horns with some gold Christmas ribbon; and Kris, the calf, had a splash of red ribbon tied to his small topknot above the middle of his forehead. They both looked marvelously silly.

Betsy put her arms around the calf while Johnny capered in the straw and shouted, "Betts, let me pat him! Lookit how his feet are uneven!"

"It's just because he's little yet," she retorted and embraced the calf so protectively that Kris bawled in protest.

"Let me pat him!"

"Well, pat him just once."

Johnny stroked the calf's nose, put his own cheek

close to the tawny one and said, "Oh, moo-baa, yourself!"

"I've got to get to work," said Mom, "or you people won't have a smitch of dinner."

Back at the house, she shooed Betsy and Johnny outdoors to play. "Keep out from under my feet or you'll be stepped on. Avaunt, avast, the two of you."

Tish helped with Christmas dinner and the whole house was fragrant with the smell of apple and mince pie, turkey and spiced stuffing. Toby kept the kitchen wood box full, and it seemed that with every trip to the woodshed he became hungrier and hungrier, in spite of his having eaten a tremendous breakfast of pancakes and scrapple.

Then Mom made the two gallons of maple mousse for dessert and poured them into the big tin cracker can and covered it tightly. "Toby, please take this out and bury it in a deep snowbank. Heavens," she said, brushing a wild brown curl out of her eyes, "I hope it freezes by dinnertime. I should have made it yesterday and put it out overnight. I don't know what's the matter with me these days—I'm all atwitter. I think that drift by the woodshed door will do, and put it far down in."

When he had packed the cracker can under a heavy layer of snow, he broke off a twig from the windbreak pines at the side of the house and stuck it on top of the maple mousse to mark the spot. In the gray twisted boughs of the back-yard crab-apple tree, two chickadees stopped poking their beaks into the weather-ragged bark for their breakfast of grubs. Bobbing their black caps, they called cheerfully, "Chick-a-dee-dee-dee!"

"The same to you!" He grinned at their merry scrambling from one branch to another.

The icicles, melting in the morning sunlight, were dripping long crystal upside-down spires from the eaves of the house and the sheds. Beside the low milk-house, he broke the end from a long one that he could reach and put the spear of ice in his mouth. Swallowing the water, he felt his throat glitter with coldness. "Um," he said to Poke who trotted toward him from the woodshed. "Good!"

The little bell on Poke's new red collar tinkled clearly in the frosty air and she kept turning her head to see where the strange sound was coming from. Finally she sat down in front of him on the path and asked anxiously, "Merow?"

"It's you, making all that noise," he told her.

Poke said she didn't care if it was—she didn't like it.

"Never mind," Toby said. "You'll have a turkey drumstick for dinner."

Dad and Cliff and Jerry were out back of the barn, skinning the bear. Toby didn't want to think about the bear. When he did, his stomach still felt strange— as if it were a little seesaw inside him. He swallowed the last of the icicle and hurried in to the good smell of the kitchen.

Tish was sitting at the kitchen table, peeling potatoes; Mom was cutting up Hubbard squash. Ribs thumped his tail beside the wood box and barked weakly at Poke, who walked over and sat down on his front paws. Calmly she washed her face and then snuggled down and went to sleep against Ribs's chest. Ribs sighed, stretched his nose over her back, and went to sleep, too.

Mom asked, "Feel like crying, Toby?"

"What?" he asked, astonished.

"Feel like crying?"

"Gosh, no! Never felt less like it in my life. Why?"

"Then you may have the privilege of peeling three dozen little white onions," she told him with a smile. "And if you weep, don't blame me."

Tish giggled. "Want to bet you won't cry, Toby?"

He bristled. "Of course I won't cry! What makes you think I will? What's peeling onions got to do with it?" He'd never had any contact with onions other than to pull them in the garden and eat them after Mom had cooked them. He sat down across the table from Tish, and the big panful Mom placed in front of him looked harmless enough—just plain, ordinary onions. Mom showed him how to peel one and handed him the paring knife.

"What do you bet you won't cry?" persisted Tish, her eyes dancing.

"Poof," he said haughtily. "I bet you a double choco-late-marshmallow-nut-hot fudge sundae!"

"Good glory!" said Mom, leaning forward to stare at him with mock distress. "Where are you going to put it?"

"When?" asked Tish, still teasing him.

"This afternoon when we go for the sleigh ride with Windy." He attacked an onion.

Tish bent over her potatoes, pretending not to notice when he began to blink after the sixth onion. Mom hustled back and forth between the pantry and the stove, casting amused glances at him but saying nothing. He tried to fight back the tears stinging his eyes. Oh, barnacles on a bulrush! He tossed a peeled onion into the second pan and fumbled for another; although it was right in front of his face, he could scarcely see it. By his tenth onion, the tears were streaming down his face and he had to stop and blow his nose.

She took pity on him. "Toby, wait a minute. Fill the

big pan with water and peel the onions under water. Better wash your face and hands first."

"Thanks, Mom. You win, Tish," he said, dripping tears. It wasn't losing the bet that bothered him—it was his bragging when he didn't know what he was talking about. "I'm a smarty," he added with a damp apologetic grin.

"You held out longer than I thought you would." Tish smiled at him. "I wouldn't last beyond three onions."

When he had finished the peeling, Mom sent him down cellar to the canning cupboard. "Two jars of peas, Toby, and a jar of pickled beets, and sweet cucumber pickles and piccalilli, and I guess that's all. If you can't carry 'em all, bring 'em up in one of those old grape baskets."

He mounted the dim cellar stairs, howling to himself,

> *Fuzzy Wuzzy was a bear,*
> *Fuzzy Wuzzy had no hair,*
> *Fuzzy Wuzzy wasn't fuzzy,*
> *Was he?*

He nearly dropped the jars when Johnny ran into him.

"Oh-ee!" yelped the little boy who was plastered with snow. "I didn't see you!"

"Better watch where you're going. What *were* you seeing?"

"Big Chief Crazy Squirrel see heap big holly-wreath cookies!"

"Ha!" said Toby. "Fine idea, Johnny. I'm starved myself. Come on into the pantry while I put these down. Hey, Mom, may we have some cookies?"

"Yes, and bring some for Tish. Three each so you won't spoil your dinners."

"I won't spoil my dinner!" Johnny hopped up and down, flopping the tassel on his red toque. "I'll only eat three little wreaths 'cause my stomach's little underneath."

"Little like an army of squirrels," jeered Toby. "Here." He took the cooky jar from the shelf and handed Johnny three cookies shaped with a doughnut cutter and decorated with sliced green gumdrops for holly leaves and with bits of candied cherries for holly berries. He put three on a small blue plate for Tish and took three himself. "That shouldn't fill us up too much."

"Nothing could fill me up," said Johnny dreamily, munching with relish.

"Anything more you want me to do, Mom?"

"Not right now, Toby, thanks."

"Tish," he asked shyly, "would you—would you mind if I tried to draw your picture with my new pastels?"

"Why, no, Toby, I wouldn't mind." She looked a trifle flustered and lifted her hand to straighten her white hair ribbon.

"Don't touch it—you look swell just as you are." His courage came back. "Hold it, Tish!"

Her hair was rumpled and wavy and her ribbon was skew-geed as if she'd just been in a pony race. He rushed for the bookcase in the living room where he'd put the pastels out of the way of Johnny's barging happiness and Betsy's concentration on Matilda. Back in the kitchen, he sat in the straight chair near the wood box, hooked his heels on the front top rung, and balanced the pastel pad on his knees. "I don't know anything about this," he muttered.

Tish looked up at him. She had a smear of dirt on one cheek from the potato earth. "Any particular way you want me to sit?"

"No, just keep on peeling." He took his pencil from his shirt pocket and sketched her outline rapidly, her bent lovely profile, her fingers on the knife, the pan of potatoes. He wondered whether he'd ever be any good at people when all he knew really was how to draw horses. He chewed his lip, gazed at Tish, and went to work with the colored pastels.

The thin crayons felt strange between his fingers. He swallowed with nervousness. "I've got to be good sometime," he said to himself fiercely. "I might as well start now." But he knew he was terrible.

Tish kept her head toward the potatoes. Even after she'd finished peeling, she didn't move until he said, "Okay, Tish. Finished."

"How'd it go?" Mom came and looked over his shoulder. "Hmm," she said, backing up critically.

"That's all right, Toby. It's the first time you've used pastels, remember."

"Yes, Mom. I haven't managed the stroke and blend of them yet. I'm getting the feeling, though. And I will."

Mom's green eyes looked steadily into his. "I know you will." She gazed at the geraniums in their pots on the window sill, past the front yard and up the woods on the south hill. "Yes, you will, Toby, if you want to, hard enough."

"Hey, Mom," Toby said in sudden surprise, "what's the matter?"

Her eyes came back. "Nothing, Toby. But Dad used to draw and paint, too. You know the bare-looking oil painting of the North Valley Road that's in our bedroom?"

Toby gaped at her. "You mean—Dad did that? It's got all the valley! You mean—Dad?"

"Yes," said Mom, standing up straight and proud. "It *is* the valley and it's Dad."

"But, Mom, why did he stop?"

"He never has, but he won't show anybody what he's doing." Mom turned toward the stove and opened the oven door absently.

Tish jumped up from the table. "Toby, may I see what you did?"

"I guess so," he said in a daze, holding out the pad. Tish sat down on the edge of the wood box. "Oh,

Toby, the colors are lovely! Do I, honest, look that slab-sided?"

He had to laugh. "I'll do better when I've learned. Hey, let's go skiing. There's plenty of time before dinner. What time *is* dinner, Mom?"

"Noon. It's only ten. Go ahead. I'll blow the cow horn at eleven-thirty to warn you. Dad says it's safe, now that the bear is where he can keep an eye on him."

Thinking of Dad, the artist, he climbed slowly to his room and fastened the portrait of Tish on his wall with Johnny's blue Christmas thumbtacks. He'd put the fixative on later. Then he recalled he'd loaned his room to Tish, grabbed his ski pants and dashed for Johnny's room, hopped into the pants, and headed for the banister.

The night pasture hill was steep and they couldn't ski down it because of the barbed-wire fence at the bottom. But they climbed it with crow-tracks and made the top, puffing and laughing. Farther west on the hill were two large sandbanks where the Clark children had always gone to play in the summer. Now the blinding sunlight fell on the broad glitter of snow and tried to penetrate the dark pine and spruce woods that surrounded the banks on three sides.

They crow-tracked again to the top of the highest bank. At the edge of the woods to the south a mountain ash lifted its scarlet berries in brilliant flat clusters against the dark green of the pines.

"Race you down to that tree!" Tish said, dropping a pole in her excitement.

Toby waited until she picked it up. "Race you!" he yelled, and shoved off. The starry powder on the crust flew in his face as he christied to a stop by the tree. Tish was already there, her cheeks flushed and her eyes sparkling.

"I thought you were going to take off into the sky, the way your head was up, looking at it. Wonder you didn't stub your toe."

"Huh," said Toby. "You're a fine one to talk. What happened to your cap?"

"Oh, my ancestors!" She grabbed at her hair. "It must have blown off."

"We'll find it on the way back up. Race again?"

"You bet," she said happily, hauling her poles out of the snow.

She beat him down four times out of seven from both sandbanks and finally they stood beside the mountain ash to rest. Toby looked up at the red berry clusters where a small cloud of blackcaps was pecking at the bright fruit.

"They aren't afraid of us," he said. "They're too busy."

"Do you suppose they know it's Christmas?" Tish tilted her cap on the back of her head and whistled up into the tree.

"Sure. They're having their Christmas dinner now. Mountain-berry sauce. What did you think they were having—Fourth-of-July supper with ice cream? Gosh, that reminds me, I hope the maple mousse freezes, because Windy's got to have a whopper of a dish." Three crows sailed hoarsely over the river road, one after another. Tingling and warm, Toby scanned the sky. "Lookit, Tish, is the sky near those snow clouds cobalt or is it—"

She grabbed his arm and whispered, "North woods!"

"Huh?" Then he gasped.

A white shape was slipping among the dark trees: it was like a white birch moving through the pines. He couldn't believe his widened eyes. Motionless he and Tish watched, and the whiteness emerged from the shadow and became a white buck, his six-pointed

antlers like delicate branches against the green
boughs.

"Wish on him!" said Toby under his breath.

"Yes," Tish murmured, not moving her head.

The buck gazed at them across the snow, the
poised fleetness, the incredible beauty, the brief—

"I wish that I'll grow up to be a good artist," said
Toby swiftly and silently.

At that instant the buck turned in a whirl of snow
dust and bounded off through the northwest trees and
disappeared.

Tish let out her breath. When she spoke her voice
was awed. "Toby, what kind of deer was it?"

"White deer. Albino." He cleared his throat and
began to scrape the snow from his right ski. He
slammed the ski upright into the pile of packed
crystals. "They're awfully rare, Tish," he muttered.

"Have you ever seen one before?"

"Nope." He didn't want to talk. What was the
matter with girls anyway? All they did was ask questions that anybody with any sense had enough sense
not to ask anyway. He scraped his left ski. "Nobody's
ever seen one around Webster County before, but
I've heard Dad and Cliff talk about one that was seen
kitty-cornered downstate years ago. Wait till we tell
'em!"

"They won't try to shoot him, will they?"

Toby glared. "Of course not. Deer season is over

anyway. They may come up and try to get a look at him. I hope they do."

"Hey, Toby," Tish said. "What are you mad about?"

"Who, me?" He snorted and felt better. "Nothing."

"Could we—" Tish paused and looked at him. "Could we tell our wishes without spoiling them?"

Toby thought hard, trying to remember whether you could or you couldn't. He seemed to remember you shouldn't. "I guess we can tell each other but nobody else. Who'll start?"

"Let's count out."

"Okay, I'll make one up." He didn't bother to think but pulled off his right mitten and poked himself in the chest first. He glanced toward the north woods and began slowly:

> *Huckle—berry, elder—berry,*
> *Goose—berry, twine.*
> *You—tell—your—wish,*
> *I'll—tell—mine.*

The final thrust of his forefinger ended on Tish's black ski jacket. She looked at him solemnly. "I wished I'd be a good surgeon when I grow up. Or maybe just a good plain ordinary doctor. I don't know yet." She studied the snow under their feet.

Toby said fast, "I wished the same about being an artist."

"Look, Toby, let them be secrets and let's cross our hearts."

Gravely they put their left hands on the tops of their heads and crossed their hearts.

"Nobody knows but us," said Toby.

"Nobody knows but us," said Tish.

They grabbed their skis and started back up the snowbank, but were halted abruptly as the echoing blast of Mom's cow horn lifted from the valley.

"Dinner!" shouted Toby.

"Dressing and gravy!" yelled Tish.

They turned east and skied as far as they could, took off their skis, and stumbled the rest of the way to the pasture fence on the river road. Toby imagined himself a famous artist and Tish a famous surgeon and he began to whistle loudly to let off steam before he blew up.

11
Who's Got the Wishbone?

D AD stood at the head of the long dining table, the carving knife and fork in his hands, and smiled down at Mom. The children, scrubbed and combed, their faces eager, sighed hungrily. "I think," announced Dad, "I'll say Robert Burns's blessing." He bowed his head.

> *Some hae meat and canna eat,*
> *An some wad eat that want it;*
> *But we hae meat an we can eat,*
> *And sae the Lord be thankit. Amen.*

"Amen," chirped Johnny. "But that's turkey and I need the wishbone to wish on!"

"Whoever finds it will save it for you," said Dad, beginning to carve. "Relax."

"Mom," Toby asked, "may I turn on the radio and see if I can get some Christmas music?"

"Yes, please, Toby. Johnny, stop kicking your heels on your chair."

"Oh, my, those cranberry-sauce Christmas trees are pretty!" Johnny quickly changed the subject. "How'd you make them, Mommie?"

"With a cooky cutter. And I can still hear your heels."

Johnny beamed at her and reached for his glass of milk. "I am a good boy," he declared in a smug voice.

"When you're asleep," said Toby from the living-room door. He found a program of carols, turned the radio just low enough, hustled back, and slid into his chair.

The three red candles in his birch-log candlestick were burning in the center of the white linen cloth, flanked by green sprays of spruce and pine. There were heaping dishes of mashed potato dotted with the green of parsley and the yellow of butter. There waited the gold of the squash, the cream color of those onions he had peeled, the light green of the peas, the dark green of cucumber pickles, the red peppers in the piccalilli, and the dark red of pickled beets. The red cut-out Christmas trees of cranberry sauce lay on a silver plate next to the pound of homemade butter that Mom had stamped with the sheaf-of-wheat mold. And in front of Dad was the glazed brown splendor of the turkey, and near Mom stood the boat of rich, brown, fragrant turkey gravy.

Toby gazed dreamily between Johnny and Tish toward the dining-room windows. He wished he could paint everybody around the table. He wished he could paint the table and the warmth and the music and the affectionate teasing and the white world outside the windows and all the family love inside the house and the fun—

He was startled from his fervent wishing by Betsy's nudge. "Dad says please pass this on to Mom."

He came back to earth, took the plate, and handed it to Jerry Burnham. "Did you feed your calf, Betts?"

She shook her pigtails. "Of course not. Georgette fed him. I gave him a cooky for dessert but he wouldn't eat it. He dropped it in the straw and hollered."

"Betsy!" Dad was handing another plate toward her.

"But I fed Matilda, and she ate every bit!" Betts was as proud as ten mothers.

Across the table, at Dad's right, Tish chuckled.

Straightening her face, she said solemnly to Betts, "There's nothing as wonderful as children who are hungry enough from lots of fresh air, like Matilda, to eat you out of house and home."

As solemnly, Betsy replied, "That is certainly so, isn't it, Mrs. Applefeather? That is what I always used to tell my mother, and do you know what she said?"

"No," said Tish, having trouble with the giggles.

"She said, 'I believe every word of it. Air does the funniest things to people.' And it does, too!"

There was a sudden tinkle under the table and Jerry Burnham said, "Ouch!" and bent over sideways. "Hey, this isn't your picnic, Poke!" He lifted the cat gently to the floor and gave her a pat. "Begone!" He rubbed his knee and as he straightened, he bumped into Mom's elbow and they both laughed aloud. "Sorry, Mary." His homely but strangely handsome face twinkled at Mom. "Poke thought I was a tree and needed climbing."

Toby caught Dad's eyes and Dad gave him a slight nod. The nod meant that Christmas was going to be all right, that even Jerry Burnham was beginning to feel like one of the family. Toby winked back.

Poke tinkled off in short spasms because she kept sitting down and glaring around to see what was ringing. She disappeared into the living room.

"Everybody all set?" asked Dad.

"I think so," answered Mom.

"I am!" crowed Johnny as if everybody needed convincing that he was.

"Sail in," said Dad.

"Gosh, this is good, Mom!" Toby looked up in time to see Cliff slipping something under his chair and there was an immediate crunching sound—from Ribs. "No fair!" Toby whispered loudly. "*We* aren't allowed to!"

Cliff's leathery face was hurt and innocent. "Whispering at the table!" he accused Toby, and selected a cucumber pickle. "Bad manners." He turned his head toward Dad. "If it doesn't snow tonight, I am a lily of the valley."

"That," retorted Dad with a whoop of laughter, "is just about as likely as me turning into a chipmunk. You and your weather."

"Dad," protested Mom. "Your grammar—"

"Is fine, Mrs. Clark. So's this dinner. Speaking of whispering at tables, Mary, did I ever tell you why I married you?"

Mom looked at him aghast. "What?"

"So I could sing at the table on Christmas, after everybody is so full of apple pie and maple mousse they can't keep on key." He gazed soulfully at Mom, a forkful of dressing halfway off his plate. "Mrs. Clark, did I ever tell you at Christmas or any other time that I love—"

"Stop it, James," said Mom, blushing furiously. "Eat your dinner and behave."

"The way you make turkey dressing," said Dad.

"Oh, *you—*" said Mom, looking beautiful and distracted.

Toby swallowed his laughter and choked. Betts thumped him on the back. He had the same trouble every year. Dad and Mom started acting up, pretending to fight, pretending to ignore each other, having as much fun as if they were kids, too. "Thanks, Betts," he gurgled.

"I always get hiccups laughing at Tillie and Tossie," said Johnny, standing on the seat of his chair and leaning across the table toward him, "but you always get the chokes at Christmas."

"You stopped?" inquired Betts anxiously, patting him gently.

"Stopped." He found his handkerchief and wiped his eyes.

"Now see what you did, Mom," said Dad. "Gave our eldest child the giggling grief! Shame on you!"

"Making fun of my turkey dressing!" said Mom right back.

"I was not! If it doesn't get first prize at Webster County Fair next September, I miss my guess."

"Who said I was going to enter it at the Fair?"

"I did." Dad threw her a kiss. "Dressing à la Clark."

Cliff tipped back his chair and tipped it down again. "Mary, these here cucumber pickles. You never tried them at the Fair in the pickle department."

"No-o."

"Well, you ought to. I could keep on eating 'em till I fall over under my own weight of 'em."

"And the beets, Mary," said Jerry Burnham, "and the piccalilli. You ought to try those, too."

Mom smiled around the table. "I'll think about it between now and fall."

Johnny suddenly yelled, "Mom! Dad! I got the wishbone! Lookit, I got the wishbone!"

"Hooray!" said Toby. "About time."

"Mom," chattered Johnny, "what you want me to wish? What you want? A pony littler than Windy, about my size? Huh, Mom?" He gulped. "Would you fit a little pony?"

"I'm kind of big for any pony," Mom answered. "But thank you for asking. You go ahead and wish for what you want. You'll have to wait until day after tomorrow, though, when the wishbone is dry."

The little boy waved the bone in his small greasy fingers. "See, Toby? I got it!"

"You may be excused, Johnny," Dad said, "to hang it on that new nail over the wood box."

"But, Dad, there're lots of nails there!"

"Yes. The newest one is yours. Betsy hammered it up for you this morning when you weren't looking. She was pretty sure you were going to get the wishbone this year."

"How could she tell?" asked Johnny.

"I dunno," muttered Dad, glancing sidewise at

Betts, who stared at him straight-faced and blinked with both eyes.

Toby gazed anxiously out of the windows again as Johnny scuttled for the kitchen. He hoped it wouldn't start snowing until after he and Windy had taken Tish for a ride in the red sleigh. The sun was growing a trifle dim.

Johnny popped up from under the table where he'd stopped to pat Ribs on his return from the kitchen. "Cliff, will my wishbone be dry by suppertime?"

"You heard what your mother said—day after to-morrow. If you pull too soon, it'll slip and nobody will get a wish."

Johnny accepted Cliff's help of a hoist into his chair. "Thank you. Tish, may I please borrow the picca-lilli?"

Dad groaned comfortably, putting down his fork. "Mary, may I sing now?"

She nodded. "Toby, you may burrow for the maple mousse. Betsy, Tish, will you please clear the table while I cut the pie? Johnny, please turn off the radio while Dad rejoices."

"I sing baritone," Jerry said to Dad, and growled two or three notes.

"Bass," said Dad. "You start, Jerry. What do you feel like?"

"Let's try 'Casey Jones.' Or 'Sweet Adeline.'"

They were testing their voices on "Down by the Old Mill Stream" when Toby skidded out of the woodshed door for the twig of pine that marked the maple-mousse snowdrift.

The snow clouds had moved up the sky until the sun above the south hill was barely visible, a faint gold disk that disappeared and then gleamed faintly through the thickening layers of cloud. He began to worry harder about the sleigh ride. But Tish wasn't afraid of snow any more than he was. The icicles along the eaves had stopped dripping. He dug into the drift and hauled out the big cracker can. Just as he finished cleaning the snow from it, he heard Windy Foot whicker and he whistled back. Windy danced in his stall. Toby shoved the big can up against his chest. "I'll be there in a couple of minutes!" he shouted across the white yard.

Windy neighed impatiently.

12

Jingle Bells

TOBY held the large speckled blue agate dish of maple mousse up to Windy. "It's maple ice cream and I know you like strawberry, but this is better. Mom made it and it's home-frozen."

Windy thrust his nose into the dish. When he lifted it, Toby laughed, "My gosh, you've got a dirty face!" Windy rolled his eyes and jumped his hind quarters. Toby wiped the pony's face with a clean cloth. "Like it?" Windy switched. "If there's any left tomorrow, I'll let you clean out the can."

He curried the pony, brushed his mane and tail, adjusted the jingling black harness that Cliff had cut down to Windy's size. "Windy," he said softly, "this is going to be a sleigh ride!"

Tish was waiting in the front yard. Toby helped her into the red sleigh and put the new Hudson's Bay blanket over her knees. As he picked up the reins there came a flurry of waving hands at all the dining-room and living-room windows. He and Tish waved back. Windy Foot gave a tug and the runners squeaked coldly and swiftly down the valley road, the small bells and the larger bells settling into music.

"Listen," said Toby, proud as all get-out.

"I am," said Tish. "Has he ever been driven with a sleigh before?"

"I tried him out a couple of times. The sleigh slants— I didn't get it quite even when I cut it down."

"Who minds a slant? Windy runs as if he had been born between thills."

"I guess he's been born to everything." His chest was about to burst with pure joy. "Go it, Windy! Go it, boy! Excuse my dust!"

Windy went it. With his lovely harness bells and his shaft bells, the pony allowed a clanking rusty truck, a lagging sledge, a blue sedan, and a long-distance bright yellow truck, to excuse his dust. The trees fled backward and the soft snow-promising air whipped past their faces.

Toby held the reins lightly. The dapple-gray pony with his black mane and tail and his black harness, the red sleigh with its black runner supports and slender red-and-black whip with its tassel blowing backward, Tish in her black snow suit and white cap and mittens, all went together and must look pretty special. Toby straightened his back, cocked his cap jauntily on the side of his head, glanced at the white pine-wooded hills and said heartily, "Yea!"

He stopped the sleigh beside the square, directly across from the drugstore. He hoped the people going calling on Christmas afternoon noticed how handsome his pony looked. Ceremoniously he helped Tish down, put the new red pony blanket over Windy Foot. "We won't be gone long, Windy, and we'll bring you a strawberry ice-cream cone."

"In this weather?" asked Tish. "After all that maple mousse?"

"Yup. And I owe you a double chocolate-marsh-mallow-nut-hot fudge sundae for my being so smarty about the onions. But I intended to get you one any-way; so that makes two. You got room?"

"I don't know. After all that dinner, even one sounds too much. But I'll try," she added with a grin.

Up the three steps Toby opened the drugstore door. Mr. Friedman was standing behind the counter. "Merry Christmas, Mr. Friedman."

"Merry Christmas, Toby." Mr. Friedman's blue eyes twinkled as he looked at Tish. He came from behind the counter while they sat down in the wire chairs.

"What would you like, Tish?" Toby asked formally. She pretended to think hard. "May I have a double chocolate-marshmallow-nut-hot fudge sundae, please?"

Toby bobbed his head. "Of course." He glanced up at Mr. Friedman's white jacket. "Two, please, Mr. Friedman."

"Certainly, Mr. Clark," said Mr. Friedman.

Toby swallowed. Wow, Mr. Friedman had called him *Mister* Clark instead of Toby! He felt terrifically grown up and sort of scared. But he beamed at Tish and she beamed back.

In ten minutes he wished she would hurry up and

finish the first sundae, the one he owed her, so he could order the second one and relax. But she ate slowly, taking small spoonfuls of the hot fudge sauce.

Golly, he thought, Christmas dinner certainly did have a funny effect on your appetite. He didn't think he could manage another mouthful himself. "Tish, are you ready for the other sundae?"

"No, my heavens!" she assured him. "This was grand, but—"

Toby was in the middle of an enormous sigh of gratitude when the door of the drugstore slammed against the candy counter.

Mr. Friedman exclaimed, "Dick!"

"It didn't bust anything, Mr. Friedman," said Dick Norton, panting. "It just slipped out of my mitten. Toby! Windy Foot!"

"What's the matter?" Toby and Tish were on their feet.

Dick tried to catch his breath and closed the door silently. "A bunch of kids—piled into the sleigh—and started licking him—he's running away!"

"Which way?" Toby bolted for the door, Tish behind him.

"Around the square," cried Dick. "Wait for me!"

From Mr. Friedman's steps Toby saw Windy racing around the farther corner of the square. Some kid was standing up in the red sleigh, slapping the reins with one hand and with the other lashing Windy Foot with the whip. He'd scrub that boy's face in snow, he'd scrub it hard.

Three other kids were hanging onto the sides and back of the sleigh and yelling. As Windy dashed around the corner, the sleigh swerved on the icy road and tipped dangerously. It didn't quite turn over, but it tossed the howling boys out and sent them sprawling into a snowbank.

Toby shot from the steps toward the roadway and tried to whistle Windy's whistle. His mouth was dry as sawdust and no sound came out. He licked his lips and shouted, "Windy!" He waved his arms as the red sleigh came tearing down the store street toward him. Windy's black mane was flying, the scarlet blanket was gone, Windy's eyes were wild with terror.

Toby whistled loudly this time and began to run frantically beside the pony. "Windy! Whoa!" The pony's heels kicked ice and snow backward. Toby whistled again and this time Windy heard him. He turned his head and nearly sat down in the thills as he braked his speed. The bells rang crazily.

Toby reached him with a gasp. "Oh, Windy!" he half sobbed. The pony was covered with lather and his sides were heaving. Toby flung his arms around his neck. "Whoa, Windy! Easy, boy!"

Tish and Dick appeared. "Is he all right, Toby?" She patted Windy's side.

Windy trembled. "He's cold," said Dick. "Wait a minute—I see his blanket across the square—I'll go get it." He rushed back with it. "Toby, the boys are coming this way, making snowballs."

"Let 'em come," said Toby. "Dick, please take Tish into Mr. Friedman's, out of the way. Here, I didn't have time to pay him. I'll take Windy to the stable for a rubdown. Meet you there."

"Okay," said Dick. "Come on, Tish."

Toby tossed the blanket into the sleigh and hopped in himself. He turned Windy around and faced toward the stable and home. "Windy," he shouted, suddenly dodging a barrage of snowballs, "dust!" He wondered what ailed those boys. Windy sailed to the livery stable.

He told Mr. Bronson what had happened and Mr. Bronson helped him rub the pony dry, not saying anything.

Finally he asked, "Mr. Bronson, what do you think made the kids pick on Windy?"

"Ain't you got any idea?"

"No, I haven't."

"You know 'em?"

"Sure. They're all in my class at school. When they were firing snowballs, I got a good look at them. But I still can't figure out—"

"Huh," said Mr. Bronson, giving Windy a reassuring slap on the rump. "You ain't got any more sense than heaven gave crickets. I happen to know that every boy in this village or out of it is crazy about Windy.

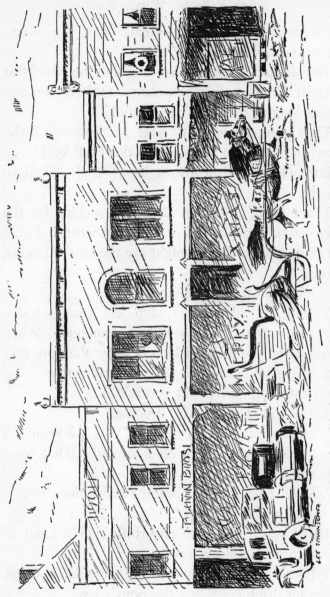

Windy's black mane was flying, the scarlet blanket was gone.

And here you drive to school every day, big as you please, and never offer 'em a ride."

Toby leaned back against the stall boards. "But gosh, Mr. Bronson, they're welcome to drive him any time as long as they don't hurt him!"

"They don't know that," said Mr. Bronson flatly. "How they going to know if you don't tell 'em?"

"Barnacles!" said Toby, aghast. "I should have thought."

"That's right," said Mr. Bronson, reaching for the curry comb. "And on top of that, you went and shot that there bear, and you might say the kids're kind of jealous."

"Well, I had to shoot the bear."

"Ei-yup, but that don't stop 'em from wishing they was you or Buffalo Bill or somebody. When school starts, you'd better let 'em know they can take turns driving Windy during noon recess or something. You'll have to figure it out yourself."

"Yes, I will. Thanks, Mr. Bronson."

"Welcome," said Mr. Bronson. "Was a boy myself once and I ain't forgotten *all* I learned. Didn't come easy, either."

Tish and Dick pushed open the stable door, stamping snow from their boots.

"Hi, Windy!" said Tish cheerfully, holding out an ice-cream cone. "Strawberry!"

"Whoosh!" said Windy and the cone disappeared, ice cream dribbling down the pony's jaws.

Toby laughed unevenly and wiped Windy's chin. "You old idiot for strawberry!"

Windy tried to eat Toby's cap.

"That horse sure likes you," said Dick enviously. "The kids went off and had a snowball fight in the square with each other, Toby. You driving out my way?"

"You bet," said Toby. "You want to drive, Dick?"

"Do I!" Dick beamed. "Know what? My pop says if our mare foals this year, maybe he'll let me raise her colt. Won't that be something?"

"It'll be great!" Toby caught Mr. Bronson's eye.

Mr. Bronson shoved his ancient cap on the back of his head and gave Toby a profound wink of approval.

"It's starting to snow," said Tish, helping with the harness.

Dick drove out to the edge of the village and stopped Windy where his own road went up a hill. "Much obliged, Toby. See you after New Year's."

"Hey, can't you come out and go skiing?"

"Nope! On account of what I got for Christmas!" yelled Dick, already halfway home.

"What'd you get?" shouted Toby.

"Baby sister! Named Squawk, so far!" hollered Dick happily.

Tish burst into laughter. "Congratulations!" she cried.

Dick waved and plowed on up the hill as fast as he could make it.

"That's something," said Tish, giggling. "Here we've been too busy to ask him if he got what he wanted, like a bike, and he turns up with a sister!"

"He sounds as if he likes her," Toby chuckled. "He sits across the aisle from me in school and every time I stand up to recite he kicks me in the ankle. Friend of mine."

"So I noticed," chortled Tish.

Windy Foot and the red sleigh were carrying them back home through the slanting snow. The small bells on the harness and the larger bells on the thills jingled in different notes and made a bright gay music through Christmas afternoon.

13
Unexpected Ravine

WHILE they were unharnessing Windy, Tish suggested, "Let's go skiing again. There's plenty of daylight yet and Jerry and I will have to leave tomorrow morning."

"I've got to do chores first," Toby said, "but you go ahead and I'll be up the hill later. I wish you didn't have to go home. Can't you talk your father into staying longer?"

She shook her head. "Not Jerry. He wants to get back to the horses. And when he's made up his mind to go somewhere, he goes."

"But why do you have to go?"

"Well," explained Tish, "Mrs. Ed is taking care of Billy Blue and Ed, but I help her as much as I can, and Jerry sort of needs me around for company."

"Yes, I know. Oh, darn it."

"Anyway, we're catching the early morning train."

He patted Windy into his stall and fed him. "No more ice cream today, boy." Windy didn't care. He was tired. "Come on, Tish, let's go tell Mom you're going skiing by yourself so she won't worry."

Mom was in the living room with both Poke and a book in her lap, gazing dreamily out of the windows toward the gentle snow. Dad was asleep on the davenport, *The Old Farmer's Almanac* moving peacefully up and down on his chest. Jerry Burnham sat in one of the armchairs by the fire, gazing thoughtfully at the birch and butternut logs.

"Hi," Toby said softly.

Jerry looked around. "Hi," he said as softly.

Mom smiled at them out of her green eyes. "How was the ride?"

"Wonderful," said Tish. "The next time I make a bet with Toby about peeling onions will be the day. Trying to finish that chocolate-marshmallow-nut fudge sundae nearly finished me."

"Tish is going up for a last ski, Mom," Toby said, "and I'll go up after I finish the chores. Will Dad mind if I'm late for milking tonight?"

"I guess not, for once."

"Gosh, Mr. Burnham, I wish you could stay over New Year's."

"So do I, Toby. It's been a fine Christmas. But we've got to get home and attend to things."

"Yes, sir, I understand, but I still wish you could." He turned to Mom. "Where are the kids?"

"Asleep," said Mom, glancing affectionately toward Dad. "Even Cliff is taking a nap. He and Dad were up all night with Georgette, you know."

As if he knew she was looking at him, Dad snored

loudly and turned over, knocking the *Almanac* to the floor. Tish hurried to pick it up. "Where'll I put it, Aunt Mary?"

Mom giggled. "Back on his chest sideways. He'll be looking for it when he wakes up. You'd better start skiing so you can get home before dark."

"I'll meet you up on the sandbanks as soon as possible, Tish," Toby said. "Party tonight, Mom?"

"Of course," said Mom. "With music."

Jerry Burnham grinned. "Tish, no high flying."

"Nope, Jerry. Don't you worry." Tish headed for the woodshed and her skis. "See you later, Toby."

When he crow-tracked up the night pasture hill, the snow was falling more heavily and it was a grand late afternoon, half warm and half chill. Toby loved the feeling of the flakes on his face and sang under his breath, "Put 'em up solid, lad, they won't come down!" When he reached the top of the first sandbank, he hollered, "Hey, Tish! Ooh-hoo!"

There was no answer. He shouted again and thought that maybe he'd missed her on the way up; so he skied down to the mountain ash. No Tish, no reply. He began to get worried. Where was she? She'd yell back if she heard him. Darn it, it was growing dusk. He climbed to the top of the sandbank once more and over to the second one near the woods. "Hey, Tish, where are you?"

The white slopes and the darkening woods mocked

him. Then he discovered her ski tracks heading off toward the north woods where the wishing deer had been this morning. "Tish!" he shouted, and shoved off. She didn't know about the ravine, the deep gully that was down there, five hundred yards in from the edge of the woods. Oh, my gosh! He skied as quickly as he could between the trees to the edge of the ravine and peered through the flakes. He filled his lungs and bellowed, "Tish!"

From the bottom of the ravine a faint cry answered him.

He knew this plunge as he knew his own hand, and he didn't dare attempt it on skis in this faint light. He took off his skis and stuck them and his poles into the snow by a pine, making sure of their location. "Coming!" he cried through his hands, and he started down on his feet. He slammed into boles and rocks and cracked his shin again and wondered briefly if the seat of his pants was still on him. When he reached her, he was sweating and terrified.

She was lying on the edge of the frozen mountain stream, her skis in a strange position. "Tish!" He knelt down. "You all right?"

"Here," she said in a strangled voice.

"What is it?"

"I've busted something." She began to cry and swallowed angrily. "Sorry, Toby. I didn't know where I was going."

"What, Tish? Where do you hurt?"

"My left leg."

"Oh, barnacles on a bulrush!" he said. "Let me get your skis off." He got the right ski off and then very gently the left one and eased her leg into the snow. She gasped once and fainted. He took his Mackinaw off and covered her as well as he could. "Tish, can you hear me?"

She made a slight sound. "Listen, I'm going home for help as fast as I can. You keep warm and don't go to sleep. Be back in nothing flat." He hated to, but he shook her by the shoulder. "You hear me? Keep awake."

"All right," she said weakly. "Hurry up."

He scrambled up the steep bank in the near dark, found his skis, and headed toward home. He wasn't allowed to ski down the pasture hill, never had been. But he recalled where the snow had drifted farther toward the south where he could jump the fence and with luck land in the river road before he ran into the stone wall on the other side. And with luck, if he could keep on going he could jump the stone wall, too. And this was no time to worry about forbidden hillsides. He knew that Dad and Mom would understand that this was an emergency. He had to make both jumps and no fooling and make it home cross-lots as fast as he could go. It was growing darker and there lay Tish helpless and in pain. He shivered briefly and took off.

He hit the front yard in a smother of snow and yelled, "Mom!"

Betsy opened the door. "Why, Toby Clark, what did you do with your jacket?"

"Never mind," he said breathlessly, wiping snow from his face. "Mom!" He told her quickly what had happened.

"Go out to the barn and get the men," said Mom. "Betsy, go upstairs and get those heavy blankets from the closet. I'll phone the doctor and get a thermos of cocoa ready. Johnny, find the thermos. Yes, and a hot-water bottle." She was already on her way to the phone. "And you, Toby, put on your old Mackinaw."

Toby made the barn on the run, forgetting the Mackinaw, and poured out the story to the men.

"Let's think," said Dad, frowning. "How are we going to get her out of that place? Oh, I know—northeast entrance to the ravine—it's the best way to get in and out."

Jerry Burnham looked as if he had been hit. He grabbed Toby by the shoulder and swung him around. His face was the color of paper. "What's happened to my little girl?"

"She thinks she's broken her leg, Mr. Burnham. And it looks like it." Toby stood up as straight as he could and looked squarely into Mr. Burnham's eyes. "We've got to get there quick. It's cold in that gully."

Jerry Burnham choked, recovered himself, and said, "All right, Jim, let's go. I can carry her easily if you'll furnish light so I can see where I'm going."

Cliff said, his eyes steady, his jaws rhythmically

chewing wintergreen gum, "Well, let's not go off half loaded. What's your mother's idea, Toby?"

"Blankets, hot-water bottle, thermos of hot cocoa. She was phoning Dr. Bill when I came out."

"As I was saying," said Dad, "the best way into and out of that ravine is from the northeast, and she'll have to be moved carefully. Toby, go hitch Windy Foot to the wood sledge."

Toby ran. "Come on, Windy. Back up. Hurry up. This time, boy, we've got to dust but fast."

Windy was rested and delighted to move fast.

They loaded the blankets onto the sledge.

"Toby Clark," said Mom, hustling him into his old faded Mackinaw, "you want to catch your death of cold?" She handed him the thermos and the hot-water bottle wrapped up in an old blanket to keep them hot. "Give her some cocoa and put the hot-water bottle on her stomach when they get her onto the sledge," Mom directed. "And, Jerry," she added, "you stop having fidgets. The doctor's on his way. He'll be here by the time you get back. You hang onto these flashlights."

Jerry seemed to calm down under Mom's bossing. "Okay, Mary. Thanks."

Cliff stayed with Windy and the sledge at the northeast entrance to the ravine. Toby led the way through the deep snow with one flashlight, Jerry and Dad carried blankets and the thermos.

"Oh, heck," groaned Dad once, "why didn't we think of snowshoes? Can you see all right, Jerry?"

"Yes," said Jerry in a grim voice.

"Hey, Tish!" shouted Toby through the flakes that slanted ahead of his flashlight beam.

"Tish!" called Jerry Burnham, stumbling through the snow.

"Keep in line," said Dad sharply, "so we'll have a clear trail coming out. Kick as much snow out of the way as you can."

Toby thought Dad was talking to him until he realized that he was the one breaking trail and that Dad was talking to Jerry. Nevertheless he kicked more snow aside and hollered again.

This time there was a voice to his left, small but determined. "Hi," it said.

"Oh, Tish!" said Jerry Burnham and stumbled toward her.

"Come on!" said Dad. "Everything's under control. Here, Tish, drink some of this cocoa. And, Jerry, we make a chair seat with our hands—remember how?" He tossed his blanket to Toby. "Wrap her up."

"Hi, Pop," said Tish, shuddering from the hot cocoa.

"Pop," said Jerry, trying to wrap his blanket around her and botching it in his anxiety. "She never called me that before in her life. Hi, baby."

"Take it easy on that leg, Jerry," said Tish. "Too bad you can't shoot me like they used to horses, but then—" She got the giggles that were mostly sobs and fainted again.

"She's unconscious," Jerry said, his voice tight with worry.

"Good; then she won't feel the move," said Dad briskly. "Toby, wrap the blankets around her shoulders and we'll pick her up. Take the thermos and the flash and go ahead so we can see. Ready, Jerry?"

"Ready, Jim," said Jerry, bending to help scoop Tish up.

When Cliff saw them coming, he shot his flashlight ahead and Windy Foot nickered impatiently. Tish came to when the sledge started. She was wrapped in all the blankets, and Toby had put the hot-water bottle on her stomach, as Mom had advised, and in spite of the sledge's up-and-down struggle out of the gully, she appeared to be feeling better. Toby just wished she wouldn't pass out any more: it scared him when she didn't seem to be breathing.

Dad and Jerry Burnham walked beside Tish at the back of the sledge, trying to ease the bumps. Toby and Cliff sat in front, Toby driving Windy Foot and Cliff shooting both flashlights ahead and chewing gum a mile a minute. Nobody said anything until at last they reached the river road and smooth going, and then Toby called, "Dust, Windy!"

The doctor's car was in the front yard, halfway up a snowbank.

"He must've gotten here on one tire," said Dad tersely, and then shouted, "Mom!"

The door was flung open and Mom and Doctor Bill and Mrs. Bill, who was a nurse, came out.

"Hello, Tish, my girl," said Mom, taking Tish's hand for a moment. "Kitchen couch, Jim. Everything's ready. Mrs. Bill, Doctor Bill, this is Jerry Burnham, old friend of ours. Toby, you go attend to Windy Foot. Cliff, will you take care of the cows?"

Toby hustled Windy into the stable, fed him, gave him a hasty pat, and rushed for the house. Windy thundered his heels indignantly at such abrupt treatment and Toby called back, "See you later!"

He opened the woodshed door cautiously. Doctor Bill and Mrs. Bill were bending over the couch. Mom and Dad were standing beside Jerry, who was sitting in the rocking chair. Dad motioned him toward the living room. Noiselessly Toby hung up his old Mackinaw and tiptoed through the kitchen. Maybe he should have gone to the barn with Cliff, but he could no more have stayed out of the house right now than he could turn into a—a painter in oils overnight.

In the living room Betsy and Johnny sat on the davenport, staring at the Christmas tree. Matilda and the alphabet book lay between them, the doll ignored, the book open to B—bear.

"Toby!" whispered Betsy.

"What?" said Toby quietly.

"How is she?"

"Dunno yet." He found his book about painters, sat down near the fireplace. "Lookit, you two. Keep still.

Doctor Bill's setting her leg and he doesn't want any disturbance."

"Toby," Johnny's voice went up in anguish, "is she going to die?"

"Of course not, stupid!" He was pretty exhausted but he had to explain. "It'll hurt for a month or so and then it'll heal. It'll be as good as new if not better. And *nobody* is to lean on her left leg, understand?"

"I'm not deaf!" said Johnny angrily, reaching for the alphabet book.

"I'm not, either," said Betts, shaking Matilda.

"Aw, I didn't mean to sound so cranky," said Toby, opening his own book and seeing nothing.

He swung his legs over the arm of the chair and gazed at the tree, himself. It had been a beautiful tree. Johnny muttered to himself over the alphabet. Betsy dressed and undressed and dressed Matilda. Nobody said anything to anybody. Toby got up and threw another log on the fire. The radio, turned low, sang "The Last Time I Saw Paris."

"P—for Paris—" began Johnny.

There was a sudden yelp from the kitchen. It came clearly into the living room. Betsy's face went white. Johnny's freckles stood out worse than they had when he slid down the banister. Toby's stomach turned a handspring. All three of them looked at each other and started to their feet. Then Toby remembered and told the young ones quietly, "We're to stay here."

They stayed there. The radio didn't help. Neither

did the alphabet or Matilda or the book on painters or the Christmas tree.

"Toby," Betsy ventured.

"Huh?"

"I wish she was our sister."

"Me too."

"Me too," said Johnny. "What'd you have to let her go skiing in a snowstorm for?"

"Did I invent the weather?" asked Toby, and stalked around the bookcases hunting for the book he had in his hand all the time. He sat down again with a thump and glared at Leonardo da Vinci.

Doctor Bill startled them. "All over, kids," he said sympathetically. "Broken leg, one cracked rib, that's all. Good thing she didn't hit her head. That girl's got the courage of ten horses. Leg's set, rib's strapped, and she's beginning to thaw out."

"Whew!" said Toby.

The doctor nodded his gray head. "Betts, Johnny, you may go and peek in, but don't talk to her. I want her to rest for a while."

The young ones streaked for the kitchen. Toby looked at Doctor Bill. "She all right? She didn't get too chilled?"

"She's all right. If you hadn't found her and rushed help to her, I don't know what would have happened. And if Windy hadn't gotten through that northeast end—I know that gully from when I was knee high to a grass blade. Let's swing this furniture around, Toby.

I want to move this davenport so that she can see what's going on tonight."

"Sure, sir, but—"

"But nothing," said Doctor Bill. "My guess is that she'll want to join in when she's rested. Tish hasn't had much family fun in her life, and a party's a party, leg or rib or whatever. I'm keeping her quiet, but she can still watch. Come on, grab that end!"

Toby grabbed his end of the davenport. "You bet!'

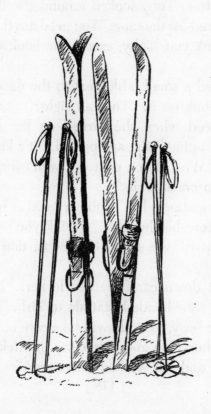

14
Christmas Night Party

LATER, when Tish was settled on the davenport near the tree, Toby looked around the living room cleared for dancing. "You need anything, Tish?"

"No, thank you, Toby, except the book your father gave me."

He shoved a small table next to the davenport and fixed the book on it. "That all right?"

She winced when she turned on her side. "This blasted strapping," she apologized. "It's kind of hard to breathe. When I'm a doctor, I won't forget what it feels like to crack a rib."

"Not to mention a leg." Toby grinned at her. "Gosh," he said before he thought, "I think you're swell."

"I'm a sissy," she said. "Oh, Betts, don't you look pretty!"

Betts sat down carefully beside her. "Toby, Mom wants you." She handed Matilda to Tish. "Here, Tish, when we're busy, Matilda will take care of you. Toby, Mom says hurry up and help carry in pitchers of milk and things and get washed afterwards."

Tish leaned the doll against her chest. "Thank you, Betsy. Can Matilda read yet?"

"Well, not yet, Mrs. Applefeather, but she's trying."

Toby snorted and galloped for the kitchen. Girls were certainly funny. "What is it, Mom?"

"Have one sandwich to stay your stomach," said Mom. "Later you may stuff, but just now I need your help."

When he had finished helping Mom and Mrs. Bill, the dining-room table was laid out with platters of sandwiches, ham, cold turkey, olives, pickles, pitchers of milk, and pitchers of apple cider.

"Whoever's hungry," said Mom with a sigh, "may help himself. I'm not going to do another thing for one day except wash my face."

"I should think not," said Mrs. Bill. "Go ahead, Mary. I'll watch the door and the kids."

Mom hurried for the stairs.

"Hey, Mrs. Bill!"

"What, Toby?"

"Is Tish going to be all right? I feel sort of responsible for letting her go skiing by herself."

Mrs. Bill's eyes crinkled. "Tish will be first-rate in no time. No need to worry. You'd better bring some more wood in, though. Here comes somebody."

Betsy and Johnny were entertaining Tish when he got as far as the living room, and then Mom came through the hall door in a swinging green skirt and a white blouse. "Where's Dad, Mom?"

"He and Jerry are upstairs, getting themselves pretty. How do you feel, Tish?"

"Lots better, thank you, Aunt Mary."

Jerry came into the living room and hurried toward the davenport. "Well," he said, gazing down at Tish, "you know what the doctor said?"

"No," said Tish. "What, Pop?"

Jerry shoved Betts and Johnny gently out of the way and eased his long length into a chair. "He said you can't be moved for a few days; so you'll be here for New Year's after all. I've got to get back home tomorrow but—"

"Jerry Burnham," said Mom, narrowing her eyes at him, "if you aren't here for New Year's Eve, I'll never speak to you again!"

Jerry blinked. "Mary—"

"Oh, come now!" said Mom. "It won't kill you to take a couple of days off in ten—fifteen—nineteen years! If you don't get here for New Year's Eve and New Year's Day and the day after, *nobody* in this house will ever speak to you again and that goes for all the animals, too!"

Tish looked at her father's startled face, gurgled, and grabbed her side. "Oh, my ancestors, what did I go and do that for?"

"All right, I'll come back for Tish. And thanks, Mary," Jerry said, smiling.

Toby gave a whoop of joy and dashed for the stairs. At the top he landed headfirst into the middle of Dad's lean, hard stomach. "Oh, gosh, Dad, I'm sorry."

Dad pulled him up. "You might give me fair warning. Wonder you didn't land on your jaw." Dad looked very handsome in his old slack suit that he'd worn at the Fair. He looked as if he were ready for anything.

Toby grinned and sobered. "Dad, may I ask you something?"

"Shoot," said Dad. "What is it?"

Toby grabbed Dad around the middle and choked, "Oil paints. You got any extra?"

Dad's chest heaved once, and his face got red. "Your mother's been telling you things."

"Gee, Dad, it's swell—your picture, I mean."

"You'll do much better, Toby—and before very long, I think. I was only waiting until you were really interested. I'll give you the paints tomorrow. Now go take your shower—we've got guests coming." He gave him a push toward Johnny's room.

"Thanks, Dad!" Toby said warmly.

He gazed after Dad as he went downstairs. "No banisters," said Dad over his shoulder.

"No, sir!" yelled Toby.

But he forgot about the no-banister business until he hit the newel post. He got off, gave himself a biff, and walked quietly into the living room. He was famished, but he felt wonderful.

The whole downstairs was filled with music and

with valley people. All the families from North Valley Road were there, talking about cakes and corn, bread, cows, and silage, the best way to make turkey dressing, and the best way to salt young cattle. Betsy was showing off Matilda's carriage and taking nicks out of people's legs and saying she was sorry and going right on running into legs. Johnny, in his Indian suit, was sitting beside Tish, singing to her. Tish looked pale but game.

"Hi, Tish. Feel all right?"

"Oh, yes! Listen to Cliff and his harmonica! And look at Jerry dancing!"

"When you get tired, yell."

Cliff with his mouth organ and Doctor Bill with his shouting kept the square dances going. Betts changed the records and Johnny went to sleep behind the Christmas tree and woke up saying that he'd never take a nap again as long as he lived.

Toby looked around at the dancers. Mom and Dad were dancing together as if they hadn't a care in the world, and they were beautiful, Toby decided.

Then he remembered his promise to Windy Foot to come back and see him. He slipped out, lit a lantern, and headed for the stable.

Windy Foot heard him coming. The tattoo of the pony's hoofs welcomed him as he shook the snow from his shoulders. He hung the lantern carefully on the nail near Windy's stall, and said, "Hello, boy."

Serena and Jake and Tillie and Tossie were asleep.

"Everything's fine, Windy."

Toby blew on his hands to warm them before he put his arms around Windy's neck. Windy neighed softly.

Toby stroked the Shetland's nose. "Everything's fine, Windy," he said. "Tish is going to get well and she'll be here for New Year's and so will Jerry, and Dad and Mom're dancing, and the kids are asleep, and what more do we want?"

Windy rolled his eyes.

"It's too late for ice cream," said Toby. "And besides, Tish and I saw the wishing deer."

Windy nuzzled his shoulder.

Toby chuckled. "But I'd rather have you."

Windy was sure of it and whooshed in Toby's hair.